Xander

Part Two, The Present

Rockstar #14

ROCKSTAR

Bestsellling Author
Anne Mercier

Xander: Part 2, The Present
Rockstar Book 14
© 2018 Anne Mercier
All rights reserved.

ISBN: 978-1724802019

Cover Image: Sara Eirew at Sara Eirew Photography.
Editor: Nicoley Baily of Proof Before You Publish.

The use of actors, artists, and song titles and lyrics throughout this book are done so for storytelling purposes and should in no way be seen as advertisement. Trademark names are used in an editorial fashion with no intention of infringement of the respective owner's trademark.

PERSONAL NOTE: The only pirates I like are Johnny Depp as Captain Jack Sparrow and Captain Morgan which means should I'd appreciate if you'd keep my books to yourself. Pirating shows a clear lack of respect for the author—me. I'd rather not meet you on bad terms, so let's not do that, let's not meet that way. Let's meet at a signing or conference instead, or let's go have a cup of coffee or a drink. Thank you for respecting the time and effort put into each book. I appreciate it very much.

AUTHOR'S NOTE

I'd like to thank you being so incredibly patient while I battled health issues as well as a bout of writer's block. I hope you enjoy the book.

It still starts with the past (BL or Before Lucy). It's only when we get to "The Present" that it's AL or After Lucy. There needed to be more of the past so I could show you everything they went through—all of them—to get from there to here. If I "told" you rather than "showed" you, you wouldn't have understood as clearly.

Also, there's an update to Xander: Part 1. So, if you have a copy of Xander Part 1, please download the update (the how-to for some of the retailers is on my website: https://AnneMercierAuthor.com/How-to. It basically removes the Epilogue from Part 1. The Epilogue was vague and nonspecific and came across as harsh, so I removed it and implemented it into Part 2 as the more detailed Prologue.

It's highly recommended to read Xander: Part 1, The Beginning, before reading Xander: Part 2, The Present; possibly even rereading to refresh your memory. I'd also suggest rereading Interlude as some of that relates to the continued past of Tera, Xander, and all of Falling Down.

It's Tera's turn to give you her side of things. I know you all love Xander, but he's far from perfect—no one is perfect. Through this book I've wanted punch one or both of them in the face multiple times. Kleenex is advised via the early readers.

The next book in the series will be Refrain, Rockstar Book 15, Ethan and Lincoln's story (m/m).

I hope you enjoy this latest installment to the Rockstar series as I did writing it. It feels good to have Xander and Tera finally get their happily ever after.

Happy reading!
Anne xoxo

PS—Be sure to keep an eye on my website, Facebook page, Twitter, or Instagram for updates. Sign up for my newsletter to be kept up to date on all things Anne Mercier.

Xander: part 2, the present

ROCKSTAR BOOK 14

It's eleven years later, and we're still living separate lives. While I know she isn't comfortable with my lifestyle after everything she's been through, I can't be without her anymore.

I need her.

She's my wife.
She's my heartbeat.
She's my every breath.
She's my everything.

I want to know every detail of her life. I want to be part of it all. I want to work as hard to get there as she did to get here.

She's always been my girl—even at the age of eight. As I face her now, there's no doubt she'll be mine until I draw my last breath.

It's time for our forever to begin.

La Famiglia

Giovanni Russo 💍 Carlotta Russo

James Kingston
Hillary Kingston (D)

JanaLee (Jana) Kingston (D)

Jenifer (Jeni) Kingston

James Benjamin Kingston

Nicole Harper Kingston

Anthony Russo
Regina Manzini Russo

Joseph Anthony Russo

Luciana Antonia Russo Kingston
Jesse James Kingston

Killian Matthew Kingston   Konnor Anthony Kingston   Kierah Carlotta Kingston   Kaid Lorenzo Kingston

Sydney Julius (D) 💍 Jace Warner — Summer Stephens

Kadence Warner

Lorenzo Russo (D)
(Giovanni's brother)
Francesca Marcello Russo

Lily Russo Manzini (D)
Tommy Manzini (D)

Joan Wathey
Rose Lynn Stewart (D)
Cage Alexander Nichols

Serafina Rosalie Manzini Nichols

Lilyana Rose Nichols (D)

Ernesto Lorenzo Russo
Vivianna Barone Russo (D)

Nico Russo

Bella Russo

(D) = Deceased

ROCKSTAR SERIES

Russo Famiglia
Giovanni Russo
Carlotta Agostini Russo
Anthony Russo
Regina Manzini Russo
Joseph Russo
Lilyana Rose Nichols(D)
Lily Russo Manzini(D)
Ernesto Russo
Viviana Barone Russo(D)
Nico Russo
Bella Russo
Lorenzo Russo(D)
Francesca Marcello Russo(D)

Manzini Famiglia
Salvatore Manzini
Pia Tratori Manzini
Abra Cipriani Manzini
Marcello Manzini (D)
Cesare Manzini(D)
Adrianna Sartori Manzini
Emilio Cesare Manzini
Thomas Salvatore Manzini(D)
Lily Russo Manzini(D)
Massimo Fausto Manzini
Contessa Fiori Manzini
Vinny(Guard)
Angelo(Guard)

Blush
Luciana Russo Kingston
Serafina Manzini Nichols
Jace Warner
Megan Melody
Trace Styx

Blush Babies
Nicole Harper Kingston
Jake Ingrassia

Lucy's Employees
Spencer Clarity
Simone Delacroix
Carmen Mahoney
Celeste Sergeant
Misty Castillo(D)
Dr. Kane Donovan

Doctors and Nurses
Dr. Matthew Mackenzie
Nurse Toni
Nurse Elaine
Dr. Taqneesh
Dr. Peerson
Dr. Felton
Nurse Sandy Baker

Nichols Records
Cage Nichols
Damian Black
Joan Wathey
Marta Shemeld
Amanda Owens
Dave Johnson
Gina Marsh
Marci Benson(D)
Alex(BFD Road Crew)

Warner
Jace Warner
Kadence Warner
Summer Stephens
Sydney Julius (D)

Burners
Lucian Cordero
Justin Harms
Gage Daniels
Kael Daniels
Mack Brookes

Falling Down
Jesse Kingston
Ben Kingston
Ethan Ashcroft
Xander Mackenzie
Kennedy Caldwell
Lincoln Ramirez

Kingston
James Kingston(D)
Hilary Markson Kingston(D)
Jenifer Kingston
JanaLee Kingston(D)
Kierah Carlotta Kingston
Killian Matthew Kingston
Konnor Anthony Kingston
Kaid Lorenzo Kingston

Security
Frank Russo
Max Bellomi
Mike Grimaldi
Gio Nasato(D)

Tattoo Artists
Harley
Bret
Hunter

CFD Employees
Mr. and Mrs Martinez
Victor

Other Characters
Carmine Pascal(Photographer)
Luther(Photographer)
Mrs. Stromboli(Baker)
Whitney whore
Heather(one of the "regulars")
Carlo(Bartender)
Noel(Guard)
Lucky(Guard)(D)
Layla Harper
Kimberly(D)
Roberto(D)
Irene McPherson(Agent)
Mel Tierney(Director)
Aiden Jensen(Actor)
Amanda Digby(Actor)
Ian Marston(D)
Dave Richardson(Reporter)
Margo Phelan(Reporter)
Mr. Leonard(Reporter)
Bart(Jeweler)
Carina Tipton(D)
Javier(Bartender)

Dedication

For all the Rockstar fans.
This one's for you.

Prologue

Xander

WE'RE ON THE road again. Falling Down is kicking ass and taking names. I hate being away from Tera. Hate it. She's going through so much, so I go visit her when I can, for as long as I can. Sometimes, I can stay weeks at a time, other times it's only days. It depends on the tour schedule, and those schedules are getting more hectic by the day. Jerry keeps adding additional dates, and three months has turned into five.

After the attack, Tera was dead inside. I could see it—everyone could see it. There was no light in her eyes. She was despondent and lost. Who could blame her? I can't imagine how she felt—I don't want to imagine how she felt because if I do, I'll kill someone. That won't be helpful to her at all.

Dad talked to a friend who talked to a friend who talked to a friend, and they found a psychiatrist who would help Tera without her having to leave her apartment. They have online or home visit sessions. I don't care what it costs—I want the best for my wife and I'll do anything, pay any price, to ensure she gets it.

I die a little inside every time I have to leave. It hurts deep into my soul. I walk out the door and I leave a piece of myself behind. That piece of me belongs to her.

Speaking about Dad, when Tera moved to New York, he moved to LA to be closer to us. He just packed up his practice and started over—taking Sandy with him. She's been with him from the first day he opened his practice, and I think she'll be with him until the day he retires.

Dad and Sandy visit Tera often and stay with her some weekends when Linc's out of town and Tera doesn't have plans to have friends over. She and Shea are still best friends, and though I hate it, she and Carter Winters are still in contact. That guy got all the firsts I was stupid enough to let him take. He'll get nothing else.

Time has gone so fast in some ways and extremely slowly in others.

It's nearly a year later when Tera and I are finally able to be intimate—not sex, but holding one another, sometimes kissing—nothing too heavy. She's not ready for that. It hurts me to know what she's been through and what she's still battling every day.

Three months after she moved into her apartment post-hospital release from the attack, she told me I could fuck other people. I didn't want to fuck anyone then and I certainly don't want to now.

One night, the decision was taken out of my hands—sort of. I was drunk and stoned and partying hard with the guys. Jesse all-but pushed us out the door, and when I leaned back against the building and the girl dropped to her knees, I imagined it was Tera. I hated—hate—myself for it.

It'd been I don't know how many months and I didn't even come. Couldn't do it. The self-loathing I felt after I pushed the girl off me had me wanting to kick my own ass. I showered in the hottest water possible and let it scald me to wash off the dirty—and it was only a blowjob. I didn't even touch the chick. I wouldn't—won't fuck someone else. I just can't.

I haven't been that drunk or stoned like that again. She means too much to me.

Chapter One

Xander

I'VE GOT SO much shit on my mind, but what's topping my list is how cramped our space is—and the lack of privacy. It's getting on everyone's nerves. We're on our fourth "mini" tour and it's *really bad.* Correction—*Ben's* really bad.

"What's going on?" Jesse asks.

"Fucking Ben's puking his guts out, man," Kennedy explains.

"Jesus. How much did he drink?"

I shake my head. "I don't know. A lot. He was doing shot after shot with the guys from Burners."

"Shit. Can he even stand up?" Jesse asks, looking at his brother slumped against the toilet on the tour bus.

"I don't think so. We might have to take him to the hospital,

Jess," Kennedy answers.

"Fuck. That's gonna get out." Jesse paces. "Let's get him there. Find a car. We aren't taking the fucking bus."

"Shit, okay." Ethan jumps down the stairs of the bus to find someone who'll let us use a car.

"This is getting worse and worse," Jesse murmurs.

"It doesn't help he's hanging with those guys. They party every fucking night—and the drugs are insane," I mention.

Jesse looks up at me. "Has he been doing them?"

I shake my head. "As far as I know, just weed. Hell, we all smoke a little weed."

"I'm not worried about the weed, but the coke they've got out every night, that does," Jesse admits.

I sigh. "Me, too. Let's get through this and try to get some control when he's sobered up. Maybe having his stomach pumped will help him gain a little perspective."

"Maybe," Jesse mutters just as Ethan comes barreling through the door and jingles some keys.

"Let's go."

Jesse and I pick Ben up off the floor. He's dead weight, covered in puke, and smells like a distillery.

"Well, they didn't have to pump your stomach, dickhead," I bite out to Ben when his eyes blink open.

"Fuck. I feel like I got hit by a truck," he groans.

"Nope, just a fifth of good ol' JD," Jesse announces as he takes a seat. "We don't have to cancel the shows since they're a few days away. They've pumped you full of fluids."

Jesse continues to glare at Ben, who closes his eyes and tilts his head back.

"I'm sorry. I didn't mean to drink so much."

"How could you tell? Shot after shot without any thought," Kennedy chastises.

"You need to chill with Lucian. He's been out longer than we have, a lot longer. We've got a shit load of touring left to do, bro," Jesse reminds him.

I nod. "Yeah, man. You don't have to party like it's 1999."

Ethan snorts. Kennedy grins. Jesse chuckles.

Ben starts to laugh, but then groans instead. "Nice, Xan."

"Dude, you know I'm full of 'em."

Ethan snorts again. "You're full of something, alright."

"Funny fucker, aren't you?" I tease.

Ethan laughs.

The next day, we're back on the road.

Chapter Two

Tera

SOMETHING'S WRONG.

The dream feels real. But it's a dream so it can't be. I try to wake myself time and again, but I fail—until the first twinge of pain hits me. I sit up and a gush of warm fluid flows between my legs.

Ugh. My period. It's so different from what it was before… well, before. Now, it's so heavy all the time.

I make my way to the bathroom and feel the blood run down my legs.

Something's wrong. Too much blood.

I step into the bathtub and shout for Dad. With Linc out of town, Dad—Dr. Matthew Mackenzie—has come to stay for the weekend.

"What's wrong?" he asks.

I look down and his gaze follows.

"Let's get you out of those pants, Tera. You need to wash up," he tells me calmly.

"But—what's happening? This isn't right, Dad."

He shakes his head. "No. No, it's not. When's the last time you and Xander were intimate?"

There's no time to blush from embarrassment. I'm too panicked.

"Five or six weeks ago."

He nods. "Tera," my dad says softly, gently, "I'm sorry, but you're having a miscarriage."

I flinch. "What? But how? We were safe, and the doctors said..."

"They never did the extensive testing, and condoms are only 97% effective."

"We didn't use a condom, though. I'm on the pill. I take it every day at the same time. This shouldn't be," I say again, my breath getting stuck in my lungs. I *know* I've not skipped any pills. Since the attack, I've been pretty controlled in everything that pertains to my body. The doctor calls it obsessive-compulsive disorder due to my need to control what they took from me.

Cramps hit me hard and I bend over, clutching my abdomen.

"Hurts," I wheeze.

"Breathe, Tera. You were sick and on antibiotics for your bronchitis. Antibiotics decrease the efficacy of the pill."

Shit. I remember. I was so sick, but we were together only twice that weekend. My mind flickers back to those times. How slowly and tenderly we made love. The first time since the attack. I didn't flinch. I was finally, *finally* able to give myself to him again. It was beautiful and so poignant. It healed me just a bit more. I'm almost there. I'm almost whole again—oh, God. The cramping steals my breath.

I'm losing our baby.

I begin to hyperventilate as tears pour from my eyes and my heart hurts so much inside my chest I wonder how I'm still alive.

"Shh," Dad whispers. "It's okay, sweetheart."

"I-it's n-not! L-losing our b-baby!" Pain lances through my entire being. Was it something I did? Am I damaged beyond all hope?

"I did something wrong."

"You did *nothing wrong*. Miscarriages aren't uncommon, Tera."

"I'm defective," I whisper. "Xander deserves children. I know he wants them. What if I can't give them to him, Dad?" If I lose him... I'll lose what's left of myself.

"To find that out, you need to undergo those tests they mentioned after the attack two years ago. You do that when *you're* ready," he reassures me.

"What am I going to t-tell Xander?" I wail. I can't stop crying. I can't stop the pain. The hurt in my heart is much worse than the cramping.

"You tell him whatever you want to tell him or you tell him nothing. It's up to you. I'll stand by whatever decision you make."

"Oh, Dad," I cry, then reach out and hug him.

He holds me and rocks me side to side for a few minutes.

"It'll all be okay."

I have doubts.

He pulls back from the embrace. "Let's get you cleaned up."

The doorbell rings and I look at Dad like a deer in headlights.

"That's Sandy. I texted her since she was out shopping and asked her to pick up some heavy flow pads," Dad tells me.

"You interrupted her day. It was her day to shop and splurge." I hang my head. I'm ruining everything.

"I'll let her in since she didn't take a key."

He leaves the room and I pull off my shorts and panties, both of which are soaked in blood. I kick them to the other side of the tub and turn on the shower. I watch and cry as the red bleeds into the clear water, turning it a hazy pink. A multi-color whirl of blood flows down the drain. Our baby.

I sit down and wrap my arms around my knees.

I wouldn't be able to see it yet—the baby—but I know it's in there—in the blood, in the cramping pain, as well as the pain shattering my heart.

Swallow it down, Tera. Swallow it down and stay strong.

"Honey," Sandy says softly. "Let's get you out of those wet clothes."

I nod. I'm going to try. For Xan.

I wake to voices in the living area. They're angry—Linc's back. Maybe he lost last night? I can't imagine it. He was up against a guy he's beaten twice before. Stan "The Hammer" Jones. What a tool.

I ease up from bed and stand before the full-length mirror. I stare at myself and I don't even know who I see. The last two and a half years have been hell on earth. I survived.

I place my hand on my abdomen where my baby would be— our baby. I bite my lip as a tear falls from my eye. Telling Xander is going to kill him inside, much the same as it's doing to me.

I make my way to the bathroom and do my business, noting that the bleeding is better but not stopped. Dad said this would be like having a period. I don't know anything about miscarriage— only that it breaks your heart.

The voices are louder again and Linc is swearing. Uh-oh. Something happened.

I throw a sweatshirt over my tank top, not bothering to change my sleep shorts. No one cares. It's just family.

Deep rumbling voices become clear as I open my bedroom door. The TV is on in the background but they're talking over it.

"That fucker!" Linc shouts. "He made a promise. And after what she's just been through, this is going to kill her inside."

"I admit, it looks damning," Sandy tells him. "But we don't know the whole story. You know how the media spins these things."

"That's not the point," Linc reminds her.

"I know," Sandy agrees.

I step hesitantly into the living space. All heads turn to me, anguish written all over their faces. For the miscarriage? No. No. For whatever the media has… oh, God.

"What happened, Lincoln?" I ask, my voice small even to my own ears.

He strides over and pulls me into his bulky warmth. "It might not be anything, T."

"You just said—" I try to pull back and look to the television. Someone muted the sound—likely Dad.

"I know what I said. I'm so sorry, Tera."

I nod and start crying. "The baby?"

"Yeah," he answers hoarsely. "How are you feeling?"

"I really don't know. I'm confused about it all. I think I'm still in shock."

He nods as he presses a kiss to the top of my head.

"There's something else."

My stomach immediately knots with a sense of impending doom. I can feel it. I start to shake, my muscles weakening from fear.

"What did he do?" I ask. It can only be about Xander. Nothing else would, how did he put it? Kill me inside. There's no way to brace for this. None. I don't want to know. It's going to destroy us. I just know it.

"There are photos…" he begins.

My breath hitches and I start to vomit, holding my hand over my mouth as I run to the kitchen garbage. Linc's right there, holding my hair and holding me up. I don't trust my legs to hold me upright.

I dry heave one last time, then rest my hands on the sides of the trash can as I take shaky breaths. The shaking is overwhelming now.

"I need to rinse my mouth."

He walks me to the sink, where I rinse my mouth over and over with water, trying to get the disgusting taste out—but it's more than just that I'm trying to cleanse.

I turn and Dad and Sandy are just taking their seats at the kitchen table. I look over. Ethan.

"E!" I try so hard to smile, but he doesn't need it. He comes over and hugs me close.

"I am so fucking sorry, Tera."

I nod. I know. They're all sorry. So am I. But I have a feeling I'm going to be so much sorrier once I know whatever it is they're trying to protect me from—but there is no point in delaying the inevitable.

"What did he do, E? It's gotta be pretty bad if you're here." They just had a concert last night and a party afterward to celebrate their latest single hitting number one on the charts. "It must've been one hell of a party."

Ethan sighs. "It's not what it looks like."

"What does it look like?" I ask, pulling back and walking over to the table. Linc pulls me onto his lap. I'm shaking so hard I'm surprised they can't hear my bones rattling.

"Tera," Dad begins. "There are some photos."

I nod. "I g-got that part. I'm guessing Xander and—someone not me?"

He nods. "Yes."

I nod and start crying again. I'm so sick of crying. Always crying. But this one—this one has me holding myself tightly inside and out, because it already hurts.

"It isn't what it looks like," Ethan reiterates. "I was there."

"Again, wh-what does it look like?"

Ethan looks at his hands, then up to meet my eyes.

"We had the party to celebrate last night. We all were drinking and having a good time—we let security party with us."

I nod. "You know better."

"We do. But we were on cloud fucking nine, hitting number one, you know? We've worked so hard for that. Two albums and we made it. It's a big deal," he explains.

"I know, E. You don't have to tell me what it means to you all. It means the world to me, too."

"I know. It's just that security got caught up like we did, meaning, we had none."

"Just get it out. Please."

"The chicks were all over all of us. Me, Kennedy, and Xan weren't paying any attention. We were talking shit and doing shots. Someone had a camera. Took pics of the chicks in various states of undress—as you know."

I nod. I do know. They've mentioned it and even videoed some of it. They thought it was funny. Me, not so much.

"Well, one was sitting on the arm of the couch, her arm around Xan's shoulders, and she was—"

"She was fucking plastered against him," Linc bites out.

"Okay. But that's nothing new."

"No, but the photos are. They're everywhere. Of me, Xan, and Kennedy, with chicks hanging on us even though we didn't know they were there. We've learned it's easier to just let them try and ignore them rather than to say no, because then more come over and try—usually harder than the one before them."

"Yeah," I whisper, looking into the living room, getting my first glimpse of the tarted up, barely-dressed chick hanging over my husband's back, her head next to his, both laughing like they were meant to be doing that forever. Another photo with Kennedy glaring at the hand on his thigh, Ethan ignoring the one behind him. Xan doing shots with the guys. The girl leaning in and about to kiss Xander—if his head turned a little to the left. Oh. Well. There it is.

My stomach somersaults, my body shakes, my heart breaking as image after image float across the screen. I can't breathe.

We made love. I gave myself to him, fully, finally, after the accident. Did he really need to go out and find someone to fuck? Surely, if Ethan could make it here, he could, too. But, he's not here. He's not here explaining.

"That's a d-deal br-breaker," I stutter out. Now, I really can't breathe. I try, but there's no air. I gasp, unable to turn away from the TV. It's like I'm in an alternate universe—watching my husband on TV, in photos with that—*tart*.

"Breathe, Tera," Dad orders sternly, pulling me from wherever I'd floated off to. He presses a paper bag over my mouth and nose. "Breathe. Look at me and breathe."

I shake my head. I can't pull any air in. I can't feel my body.

"She's in shock. Thump her on her back, Linc," Dad tells him.

"No way—"

"Do it! Now!" Dad orders.

He does, pounds my back hard and I gasp, pulling in air—glorious air.

"Head down, between your legs," Sandy demands.

I automatically listen—like always. Sandy and Dad know

what's best. I feel exactly as I did that day at the shack. I feel like that young girl who's seen something she never ever wanted to see. Xander with someone else.

Only, this time, it feels like so much more than a betrayal. Not only because he broke our deal, but because of the time we spent together. Because of the things he said that night—things like he didn't want anyone but me, he'd never need anyone but me.

A sob bursts free. This is the first time I've let myself cry since before the attack—I mean *really* cry. The kind of cry you feel down to your soul because it hurts that much. This—this hurts that much.

Linc rubs my back while Ethan looks on helplessly. Sandy twists her hands while Dad keeps reminding me to breathe.

I breathe—between cries from a voice I don't recognize—yet, it's mine.

I meet Ethan's gaze, then Dad's.

"H-he l-lied."

Dad's mouth presses into a flat line.

"It's not… he didn't…" Ethan begins.

"H-he st-still lied."

Ethan swallows hard and nods once.

I didn't know who I was after the attack. I really don't know who I am now—after losing the baby. I don't remember who I was before Xander. I need to find out who I am after.

"H-he was partying, letting that… letting her… while I was losing our baby."

"This happens all the time, Tera. He didn't do anything," Ethan pleads.

I nod. "Knowing it and seeing it are two different things—especially now." I take a shuddering breath and say the one thing I never imagined I'd ever say in my life. "I don't know if there's any coming back from this. I just don't."

"Tera—" Dad begins.

I shake my head. "Ethan's here. Where's Xander? *Where is he?*"

Ethan looks at me. "I don't know."

I nod. "Me neither."

And that's pretty damning in itself.

Chapter Three

Tera

I'M LYING ON the sofa with my favorite fuzzy blanket, a box of tissues, and my favorite chick flicks. Ethan and Linc hung out longer than I expected. I mean, they made it through *The Family Stone* but they bailed when I put in *Dirty Dancing*.

Before they left, Linc looked at me over his shoulder with a cheeky grin and said, "*Nobody put's baby in a corner*. Don't you forget it, either."

Sometimes, my brother is pretty okay.

I'm so relieved Dad agreed to stay with me while Linc was out of town the last couple of days for his fight. I'd have had to go through the miscarriage alone. I can't imagine that, how scary it'd have been.

Dad takes off after awhile and Sandy joins me for some girlie movies. Sandy's been a godsend. I'm thrilled she came with Dad. Doctor and nurse, but best of friends. Their friendship is one I admire. I always have. I do regret that I ruined her shopping trip. Truthfully, I think there's a whole lot more than friendship there. There always has been, if I'm honest.

She chooses *Magic Mike XXL*. I smirk through my tears. They just keep coming. I can't feel anything. I'm numb, so how am I still crying. I suppose, my body will continue to grieve for my broken body and broken heart even though I'm working very hard to harden myself against it. The Xanax I took earlier helped some— not enough. I should've gone straight for the Valium.

I sigh inwardly. I've never abused my meds. I'm not going to start now.

There's a soft knock at the door and I look to Sandy. She's as confused as I am.

"Who could that be?" she asks, absent-mindedly. "Do you want me to get it?"

I take stock of myself. Sleep shorts, sweatshirt, hair up in a disastrous bun, glasses on, face red and blotchy from crying, and I've likely got dried snot on my nose.

"Nah. I'll get it."

I know who it is. Who else would it be? At least he didn't let himself in with his key—though, with the chain lock, he wouldn't be able to get in anyway.

I pull up my blue fuzzy socks. Yeah, I'm a real badass. My knees are shaking, my heart racing, and I can't decide if I want to cry or punch him in the face.

The third time he knocks, I unlock the three deadbolts, then the doorknob lock. Yes, I have issues. I've never denied it. I'm working on it. Don't judge.

I don't remove the link chain so I can only open the door about four or five inches. I put most of my face behind the door, giving him only my left eye, part of my face and mouth, along with my hand. That's all he gets.

"Yes?" I ask.

He looks like death warmed over.

Well, pal, that's exactly how I feel. Welcome to my world.

"Tera—"

"What can I do for you, Xander?" My tone is clipped, though I can't quite stop the quiver in my voice as I ask.

"Baby—"

"There's no 'Baby' here. Not anymore."

"Can I come in? We need to talk," he pleads.

"I don't think that's a good idea."

This is hard, so much harder than I anticipated.

"I need to explain," he urges.

"No need. Ethan explained it all," I tell him simply.

His brows rise. "He did? Ethan's here?"

I nod. "He isn't at the moment. He and Linc went out for a while." Damn good thing for him, too. Lincoln, with his current mood, would likely pound on Xander a bit—a bit for Lincoln is too much for normal people. He's a *very* big man with *very* big fists and he knows how to use them. MMA fighting is no joke—especially since he's underground.

"Oh," Xander breathes in relief. "So… if you know nothing happened…"

"Why am I not inviting you in with open arms?" I ask with snark.

"Uh, well… yeah," he answers carefully. Not careful enough.

"It's like this. We had a deal—one that I *needed* to be kept." *Especially now.* "But you didn't. You plus chick plus photos plus media," I laugh mirthlessly, "*extensive* media, equal deal breaker."

I'm shaking. I hope he can't see. I want nothing more than to tell him about yesterday, but I can't get past today.

He doesn't respond.

"It's a real good thing I kept in the background as I insisted, right? You remember. Of course, you do. It was just last week when you tried to get me to go public about everything. And, you know what, Xan? I nearly did. I was about to. I was waiting for you to come next weekend and I would have sat next to you as *Rolling Stone* interviewed us and we divulged our relationship. But now? I'm really glad I didn't. I mean, can you imagine the circus? How many paparazzi do you think would be camped out on my doorstep if they knew I was the *wife* of the rockstar drummer of *Falling Down*—especially after such publicly damning images."

He doesn't answer again.

"How many?" I press.

"I don't know, Tera. God, T, I'm so sorry. We let down our guard. We were celebrating. We worked so hard to get here," he explains.

I nod. "At what expense?" I ask, then a sob bursts free. I can no longer contain my false indifference. I fall to my knees and let out a keening wail. Not just for his lies, but for the fact I need to let him go.

He's on his knees, trying to reach for me through the few inches in the door. For a second he grabs ahold of my sweatshirt, but I pull free

"I don't have the luxury of letting down my guard. I once was carefree and that attitude nearly got me killed. But, Xan?"

"Tera..." he cries.

"I let my guard down with you. I trusted you. I trusted you to be true to our deal—to *me*, to *us*. I believed the things you said when we made love this last time, about how I'm enough. Foolish girl." I shake my head and swipe at my tears.

"No, Tera, please don't do this," he begs.

"It wasn't me who did this. *You* did this. You and Jesse and Ben and Kennedy and Ethan. You knew the stakes. Every one of you knew and you each made a deal with me."

"Please, Tera… don't…" he pleads.

I shake my head, sobbing, on my knees because my legs are too wobbly to hold me up.

"Don't you see?" I whisper. "I'm not ready for the attention—the limelight. You knew that. You all knew that. But last night, the band came first—for all of you. That was the first time I've ever felt betrayed in the nearly four years you've been doing this. If I'm betrayed by family—by my *husband*, who can I trust?"

It all comes out as a whisper, but with the way Xander recoils, you'd think it was a gunshot.

"It won't happen again, T. We talked about—"

"Stop. Please, just stop."

"No. Tera, listen to me."

"I've heard it all. You were partying and living it up, letting your guard down, letting the media into places they should never have gotten, while I was here…" *losing your baby.*

"You were here, what? What, Tera?"

"It doesn't matter. It doesn't matter," I tell him flatly. I'm in that place again, the one where reality doesn't exist. The one where only I exist. I've been here before. It's somewhere I haven't had to go for nearly a year.

"Tera!" Xander keeps shouting over and over, reaching through the door, trying to break the chain lock. It's reinforced. There's no way he'll get in without a bolt cutter.

Sandy rushes over, pulling me into her embrace, but I barely feel it. I let myself go limp in her arms and she cries out in shock and anguish.

"What the fuck is going on here!" Lincoln bellows. "God damn it, Mackenzie, haven't you done enough?"

They're fighting. With words and fists. Ethan and Dad barely able to pull them apart. I watch with detached fascination.

"Lincoln, you will stop right the fuck now!" Dad yells, and Lincoln pulls back, chest heaving, lip bloody, eye swollen, knuckles raw. I can't see Xander. I don't want to.

"Fuuuuck," I hear Jesse say.

"No," I whisper. "No. I can't. Not all of them. No."

Sandy holds me tighter. "Okay. Okay. Let's get you to your room. Then they can fight it out as much as they want."

Bed. Bed sounds wonderful. I can watch movies in my room.

"Listen up!" Sandy shouts. "I'm only letting Matthew in. *Only Matthew.* The rest of you can wait until we've got Tera settled and away from this fucking disaster." She huffs at them. "Really, boys. What the hell were you thinking?"

Sandy swore twice. She *never* swears unless she's so far past her limit she can't handle it. I hate this. Hate it all. I wish Sandy could come to the void with me.

No one responds to her. She unlocks the chain, lets Dad in, and locks the door once more.

"The only one who can get past that chain is Lincoln, and he's not going to try. Not today. Not right now," Dad tells us.

"I don't care. They can break the fucking door down if they want" I hear nothing from them. I feel nothing.

They help me to bed.

"Which movie did you want?" Sandy asks.

"*The Family Stone*, again. They're a good family."

Dad hugs me. "It'll be okay, Tera."

"M'kay, Dad."

He sighs. "She's back there, Sandy—only, for a different reason. She just got to some semblance of normal." He runs his hands through his hair as he paces the floor. "FUCK!" he yells.

At that, I jump, because Dad doesn't do much yelling *or* swearing.

"Don't swear because of me. Just—don't."

He pulls me into a tight hug. "Stay here, with us. Don't go back, Tera. Please, don't go away again."

"I can't. It's just too much. Only for a little while."

He sniffles, then whispers, "Okay, baby girl. Okay."

He gets up and hugs Sandy tight. They're murmuring to one another. He heads for the door—to deal with the "disaster".

"Dad?"

"Yeah, Tera?"

"Tell Ethan I'm not mad at him." Dad looks at me in surprise. "He showed up, Dad. He showed up when none of the others did. Not even my... husband."

That pain slices through the void. My husband. My best friends. My family.

"I'll tell him," he answers, then closes the door behind him.

Sandy comes over and wipes my face.

"Am I crying?"

She makes a sound in her throat. "Yes. You're crying."

"He's going to need you out there. Dad. He'll need your help."

She looks conflicted.

"I'll be fine."

"Did you want to take something to help you sleep?" she asks.

"No. I want to watch the movie. They're a good family." I used to have that and it all went to hell in one day. How does that happen?

"Okay, honey. I'll come check on you."

"M'kay. Thank you."

"I love you, Tera," she tells me.

"I love you, too."

I may call her Sandy, but to me, she's my second mom.

"Can you call my mom?" I ask.

"I already did. Rest now."

The door opens and the dull roar of heated voices turns into an explosion of raised, angry voices. When it closes, I'm once again cocooned in the solitude of my room. I press play on the remote and pretend that's my family on screen—that it hasn't just shattered.

Chapter Four

Xander

I FUCKED UP. I knew it. I know it—but how do I fix it? Can it be fixed?

"What the fuck just happened?" Kennedy asks, dumbstruck. He walked up the stairs to see Linc smash his ham-sized fist into my face. I'm pretty sure my nose is broken, but I don't care. All I care about is Tera.

I shake my head. "That look on her face. I've seen it before."

"Fuck," Ben mutters.

I run my bloody fingers through my hair and tug.

"I fucked up so bad. I knew better. I knew and I partied anyway."

"Dude, you didn't fuck anyone. What's the big deal?" Jesse asks.

"You broke your promise to her, you motherfucker!" Linc yells and gives Jesse a shove.

Jesse doesn't break a sweat. "You may be bigger. You may be able to kick my ass, but I'll get a couple good ones in. Push me again, Fucker. See what happens."

Jesse's a scrapper. He's been known to fight with the toughest of them. He's also been known to get down and dirty. It's no surprise he's not afraid of Linc—even if the guy can pound him into a pile of mush.

"How the fuck long have we been standing out here?" Ben asks.

"Who cares? We'll stand here as long as it takes," Kennedy replies.

Finally, after what feels like hours, Dad opens the door, but he doesn't let us inside.

"There will be no fist fighting—no physical fighting of any kind in this house. Do you understand?"

Everyone mumbles.

Dad leans forward. "Do. You. Understand?"

Now everyone is quick with their "Yes, Sir". My dad demands respect. He deserves it. He raised us all—hell, he still is.

"Jesus. Who's the worst of you?" Dad asks as he takes in our battered appearances.

"Xan," Ethan answers.

Dad shakes his head. "Christ. You're worse than when you were teenagers. Are you ever going to grow up and realize there are better ways to deal with things than with your fists?"

Damn. Not a place to go while Linc is pissed off, but Lincoln doesn't even blink.

"No, Sir. I'll fight and get all the aggression out in the ring—unless someone fucks with my family. That's what happened today."

Linc paces back and forth.

"Seeing her like that, on the floor, so broken. The light in her eyes is gone again. It's fucking gone and if you fuckers had done what you promised her you'd do, it'd still be there," he accuses, accentuating it with a pound of his fist against the table.

"You're not wrong," Kennedy agrees.

"No, I'm not. I hate that I'm not—for *her* sake. You're my brothers, but she's my sister. My twin. I will protect her with my last breath. She'll always be standing next to me—even if it means you aren't," Lincoln tells us flatly. "It's not how I want it, but it's how it is."

"This is bullshit," Ben growls. "All we did was have one night of fun without worrying about all the shit. We *deserved* that! We hit number one, for fuck's sake. That's *huge!*"

Ethan sighs. "Yeah, it's huge, man; but at what cost? Tera—our sister? Xander's *wife*? We didn't think that through—shit, we weren't thinking at all."

"Don't we get to do that? Not think—for just one night?" Ben asks.

"You saw Tera. You tell me," Jesse answers. "That's too high of a price to pay."

Ben scoffs.

Kennedy cuffs him on the back of the head.

"The fuck, man?" Ben scowls.

"Just trying to help you get your head on right," Kennedy replies.

"I'm going out for a smoke," is Ben's response—well, that and a slight door slam.

"What's going on with him?" Dad asks.

"He's going through some shit. Nothing we can't handle, Pops," Jesse answers.

"You sure?"

Jesse nods. "Yeah. If not, I know your number."

"Good. Now…"

Pain lances through my face unlike anything I've ever felt before—even worse than Lincoln's fist. It works its way up into my brain, my skull, my jaw. Fuck!

I let out a howl.

"Yeah, yeah," Dad says. "Let's get this set before it heals like that."

"Shit, Dad. Isn't there a less painful way?"

Jesse snickers. "You don't want to ruin your pretty face, do you?"

I give him the finger.

"You didn't hear me wailing like a girl when he set my nose—"

"Three times," Dad interjects.

"Whatever. I'm not as badass as you. I can admit that."

"Son, this is going to hurt me more than it hurts you," Dad tells me with a smirk.

"Lies!"

Snap, crackle, pop. That's what it sounds like as he manipulates my nose, bringing tears to my eyes and my bladder threatening to let loose.

"There. All done," Dad comments as he wipes his bloody fingers on a dishtowel. Thankfully, not Tera's fancy ones. "That wasn't so bad, was it."

Not a question. I just scowl.

"Here." Sandy cuts a tampon in half and inserts one half in each nostril. She then hands me an ice pack. "You're going to need this. It won't stop the black eyes, but it'll help with the swelling enough that you'll be able to breathe."

I look at her, then Dad. They're silently communicating—laughing at my pain.

"Thanks," I reply blandly.

Now, Dad lets out the laugh. "You fight, you pay the price."

"I didn't even start it—"

Lincoln glares at me, arms the size of my thighs folded across his chest. "Don't even go there, man."

I look down and collapse into the kitchen chair in defeat.

"What the hell were we thinking?" I ask aloud, to no one in particular.

"I don't know, but you *all* screwed the pooch with this one," Sandy berates.

"I don't even know what to do." I'm helpless.

Sandy grabs my hand. "Leave her be, Xan. She needs time to heal."

"Heal? Did something—"

"Her heart," she answers quickly—too quickly.

"Is there something else going on here?"

"She just needs time," Dad replies.

That's not an answer.

"She's gone, man," Lincoln says aloud. "She went back there."

"What?" Jesse asks.

"She went back to that space inside herself, the one where no one can reach her," Lincoln informs him.

"Damn it. I'm so fucking sorry for last night, but sorry isn't enough this time," Jesse mutters. "I knew she was fragile. She'd just found her way back to us."

"Don't beat yourself up, brother. We were all there. None of us were thinking clearly," Ethan placates.

"No, we weren't. We were too wrapped up in ourselves to re-member there are people who can and will—do—get hurt when we're careless," I add. "The question now is: How do we make things right?"

Dad shakes his head. "You can't. Not right now. She needs space."

"But, Dad, her description of space felt like a thousand miles between us," I tell him. "She sounded so final—like it was over. Everything was over. I can't let it be over. Without her…" I drop my head into my hands, dropping the ice pack. Who fucking cares about my nose? Who fucking cares about anything when Tera's not there?

"I should talk to her," Jesse announces.

"That's not a good idea," Sandy replies.

"This sucks," Jesse bites out, then looks at Sandy. "Yeah, I know. We made our own bed."

She nods.

"Ethan," Dad begins, "Tera wanted me to tell you she's not mad at you."

"Really?" Ethan asks, hopeful, eyes glistening.

Dad nods. "She said you came here, for her, first. Before anyone else."

Ethan swallows thickly and nods. "I did. I knew what… I called Linc last night and caught the first flight out."

"She knows that. She appreciates you, Ethan," Dad tells him.

I want to kick my own ass. I should have hopped on the plane. I should have left that party when I wanted to instead of letting Ben and the guys talk me into staying. I keep saying it, but I fucking knew better.

"I can't live without her. I don't know how. I don't want to learn how, either. She's my heart," I whisper.

"We'll fix this, man. Somehow, we'll fix this," Jesse encourages.

Maybe for them… but it's different for me. It's meant to be different for me. She's my wife and I didn't show her the respect she deserves. It wasn't just a "deal". I promised her… we all did.

"I think keeping Ben away from her right now would be a good idea," Kennedy tells us. He gives us all pointed looks and we all nod. Ben's not in the best place right now. He's still drinking heavily, smoking weed. Hell, we all drink and smoke a little weed here and there, but Ben's doing it like he's on a mission.

"He'll level off," Jesse assures us.

I give him a look. He knows what I'm thinking. Ben hasn't leveled off so far, what's going to get him to do so now? He's a ticking time bomb, going off on anyone who he thinks so much as looks at him wrong. He's wound tight and it's pretty fucking frightening watching Ben drink himself stupid every night.

"What do we do now?" I ask.

Silence is my answer. This is going to get so much worse before he shapes up.

Chapter Five

Tera

I KNEW I'D have to talk to him before he left. I just haven't had enough time to steady myself.

"Tera. Open your eyes. I know you're awake," Xander coaxes softly.

So I do, and I look anywhere but at him.

"I need to pee," I announce, then push him out of my way as I stalk to the bathroom.

That didn't take long enough. I wash and dry my hands, take a steadying breath, and walk back out there.

"Tera…" he begins.

I cock my head to the side. What's he going to say that's different from what he's already said?

"I'm sorry. I am so fucking sorry. I'll be honest with you. I've become so accustomed to chicks hanging on me, I don't even realize they're doing it anymore. I just let them get their five minutes of rockstar time while I hang with the guys," he confesses.

I pull my sweatshirt over my head. I'm beginning to smell. Eww.

"I know all of that, Xander. I just never thought I'd have to see it. Ever."

"I wish I could go back and undo it, T, but I can't. I'm sorry you're hurt. I'm sorry it happened. I'm sorry I let my guard down. I'm—"

"Sorry you were caught. On film. For the entire world to see."

He nods.

"This is what I was afraid of, Xander. I *knew* that if—when—the time came that you were caught in photos, it would explode. And it did. It did because you've never been photographed like that before. No one's seen you like that, so it's being made into a bigger deal than what it is. Even I know that," I admit.

He nods again.

"But... You're my husband. They're my brothers. You all made me a promise to keep *you* out of those photos, those tabloids, off TMZ. I know the groupies are part of the gig," I nod, "but you know I never wanted to see it. It's why we have the deal. It's why the guys agreed to help keep you out of the spotlight."

"I know, Tera."

"But you're in it now. Jesus, Xan. Can you imagine if we'd have had that sit down with *Rolling Stone* already? Can you imagine how that would make me look? How it would make me *feel*? I'd be a laughing stock. *This* is why we both agreed to keep our relationship to ourselves—to keep it private. It's the only thing we've got left."

"I'm sorry. I won't ask you to do anything you're not ready for. I just miss you so fucking much and I'm proud of you. I'm proud you're my wife, which is why I was excited to do the interview. I see now how exposing our private life could hurt you." He groans and tugs on his hair, much the same way his father does when he's frustrated.

"I want this life for you, Xander. I want you to live your dreams. None of that has changed."

"But…" he prods.

"But," I turn around and face him. "But, I can't be a part of it. You need to live your life and I'll live mine."

"What?" he whispers.

"You're living your *dream!* Sex, drugs, and rock and roll. *Live it,*" I encourage.

"I want *you*, Tera. You're a part of it all, you're a part of me."

Tears begin to fall and I close my eyes, only to see images of him and the band, the girls draped over them, the alcohol, the fun, while I was here losing our baby. My heart is shattered. My womb possibly too damaged to give him children. He deserves better.

I want to tell him. I *should* tell him. But I don't. I won't. He doesn't need to go through more anguish. The level of guilt he has now is too much. I can't imagine how much worse he'd feel if he knew… well, if he knew.

"Xan," I say softly. "I will always be a part of you and you will always be a part of me, but I think we need to take a break."

He flinches, shock evident. "A break? No. I don't want a break."

"Xander."

"No. I don't want a break. I don't *need* a break. All I need is *you*," he pleads.

"If that were true, Xander, we wouldn't be in the mess we're in right now."

He recoils as if I'd slapped him. I don't blame him. It was harsh—deliberately so. I need to push him away. I need him to go *live*. I'm too broken. Everything about me is broken.

"You don't mean this. You're just upset."

"No, Xan. I mean every word. We need a break."

"Who are you right now?" he asks.

"I'm Tera. I'm just showing you the broken parts I usually hide. These broken parts are all I have left. I'm not whole, and I don't think I ever will be again. You deserve *everything* this life can give you," I tell him as I hold both of his hands in mine.

He's shaking his head in denial.

"No. Tera, don't do this. I don't want this."

I sigh inwardly and bite the inside of my cheek so I don't sob. This is going to hurt so badly.

"Did you ever stop to think about what *I* want?"

Xander just looks at me, his eyes filled with despair, anguish. "You want this?"

I have never lied to him. I hate that I'm going to right now.

"I think it's best. You can go live your life and I'll live mine," I tell him, my voice hollow, even to my own ears.

"You want to see other people, you mean," he says, his lip curling a bit.

"Maybe. If that's what life brings. We were too young to know what we were doing, too young to realize that life was larger than we were and it had other plans than the ones we made."

"You don't mean this," he says, getting up to pace. "I know you don't. You can't."

I take a deep breath, look him square in the eyes, and lie. I lie my ass off. For him.

"But I do. I think we settled too young in life for what we thought was right for—"

"*Settled?* You *settled* for me?" he bites out.

I shrug a shoulder. "I don't know."

He drops his head and breathes deeply though his mouth—his nose still too swollen to breathe through. When he raises his head, the look in his eyes isn't a kind one.

"You *settled* for *me*. Is that right? I gotta tell you, Tera. I didn't see this one coming."

There he is. The pissed off Xander. The Xander who will make this easier for me—for us. I love him with everything inside of me, but this man deserves everything his life has to offer—not some broken reject who can't even give him children. No. He deserves everything.

"Settled," he chuckles, and I wait for it. Oh, this is going to hurt so much. He won't mean it, but I pushed.

He leans in so his face is right in mine. "I'm the best fucking thing that's ever happened to you, Tera Louise Ramirez Mackenzie. Settled. Are you fucking kidding me? I'm a catch, baby. I'm a fucking rockstar! I could have as many women as I want every night of the week. Settled. Give me a fucking break."

"You're wrong."

"Oh yeah? Do tell."

I'm sorry, Xander.

"You can't have *me*."

He nods and smirks, hands on his hips, as he lets out a quiet humorless laugh.

"And what's new with that, huh?" he replies.

I don't flinch—not where he can see it, but oh, does it hurt—my heart.

"This is what you want?" He's not really asking, just talking aloud. He's angry and hurt and lashing out at me—just as I knew he would.

"Is it?" he whisper-shouts.

"Yes," I whisper.

"You got it."

With that, he turns and walks to the door. He hesitates before turning the knob, not looking back.

"You're going to regret this."

He opens the door and closes it with a quiet click.

Oh, Xan, I already do.

"You idiot!" Linc yells at me.

"Shut up. You don't know—"

"Little sister, I sure as hell do. I *know.*" He paces, agitated with me—again. "Why'd you do it?"

"He deserves more than I have to give."

"That's *his* decision. And a man has a right to know about his child! Jesus. Fuck!"

"There *is* no child," I whisper, wiping the tears.

"You should have told him. It's his right as the father—as your husband. You need to tell him," Lincoln tells me, continuing the lecture.

After Xander walked out of my room, he told everyone in the room I wanted a break so he was giving it to me. He didn't want me to feel like I was *settling.* I really hate that word, now.

Then, as I watched from the doorway of my room, Xander gave me one last look before he walked out of my apartment and out of my life.

"Maybe there's something else out there for me," I say aloud. Dante's really kind and good-looking and sexy. "So what if no guy can set me on fire like Xander does—no one will ever be able to—but maybe they'll come damn close. I can live with that so long as Xander Mackenzie is out there living life, making the most out of it, and not wasting his time on the broken girl he thought he fell in love with at the age of eight. Who falls in love in grade school?" I scoff.

"You two," Linc reminds me.

"Puppy love. This too shall pass."

"Who're you trying to convince?" Lincoln asks before he grabs his gym bag and heads out the door.

Me.

Chapter Six

Tera

I'T'S BEEN SIX months since I've heard from Xander. It's what I wanted and yet, I didn't. He's moved on. I've seen him in photos, magazines, and on the gossip channels with models and actresses; gorgeous, beautiful women—but never the same woman twice.

Over the last six months, Shea's come to hang out a lot and I've focused on my painting. Dante—Mr. DiMora—had a construction crew install a stairway going from my apartment down to the studio. It's all enclosed and protected with a keypad lock. I really think he's going to too much trouble to appease my needs. He's always been that way.

When he found out Xander and I are on a break, he asked me

on a date. I looked at him and laughed. Really? I don't *go anywhere.* I can't. The second I get too close to the door, I begin to shake and sweat. It's as bad as it gets—the panic.

Agoraphobia is what my psychiatrist calls it. I call it me not trusting anyone I don't know, especially in open spaces. Some days, I can't even stand by the windows to look at the people below. I get a panicked feeling that they're staring at me, that they are just biding their time and scoping things out before they come back here to hurt me. It's those days I close the pale pink sheers. I can still look out, but up here, no one can see in.

I am a mess. My heart's a wreck. My head's chaotic. My body's damaged.

I want so much to go in and get the tests done to see if I'm able to carry children, but I don't know how that would work. How would I get there without giving myself a panic-induced heart attack or hyperventilate?

It's really a moot point right now, anyway. I'm not with Xander anymore, and I certainly don't want to have children with anyone else.

Well, that's telling, isn't it?

My subconscious mind reveals this to me a lot. But I do nothing about it. And I won't. Xander's living his life the way he's meant to—even if it's killing me inside that I'm not a part of it.

Tonight, I'm having dinner with Dante again. It's our fifth date. I've cooked or we've ordered in up until now, but tonight he's got something special planned down in the gallery.

The back part of the gallery was added on to accommodate my studio upstairs. In that section downstairs is the new office area and a small bedroom for nights the gallery shows run late.

I'm putting the finishing touches on my lipstick when I see Linc leaning against the doorjamb, watching me.

"What?" I ask, seeing the judgment in his eyes.

He shakes his head. "You're really going to do this?"

"Do what? Move on? Date a handsome man who is kind and generous? If that's what you're asking then, yes. I am going to do this," I reply, knowing full well he's asking about me sleeping with Dante. It's been a gradual lead up to this point. I know what tonight's about and Lincoln is no dummy. There's a reason we're having dinner downstairs.

"You're going to fuck him. I know you are. What I don't get is, why? Why are you doing this to yourself?" he asks.

I turn to face him. I no longer get angry or upset or, even, guilty when he asks me this.

"Have you seen the press? He's *happy*, Lincoln. He's living the life of a rockstar and I want that for him so much," I admit.

"Even if it doesn't include you?"

I nod. "Yes. Even if it doesn't include me."

"You're an idiot."

I just sigh.

"You think he's happy?"

"I do. His smile isn't faked. It's genuine, Linc. You see it as well as I do. He hasn't smiled like that in so long, not one of *those* smiles."

"And you think that has to do with you being here and him being there. Him doing whatever with whomever and vice versa."

I nod.

"I've talked to Ethan a lot. Xander isn't as happy as you think he is. He still worries about you whether you allow him to be here with you or not—and because he's there and you're here, he worries even more. He calls me, T. *Me*. To find out if you're okay," Linc informs me.

"I know. I'm doing just fine. I hope you tell him that."

"I do. I lie for you."

I shake my head and he holds up a finger.

"Don't lie to me. I know you, Tera. I know you as well as I know myself. You're miserable on the inside. You want him here with you, but you think he's better off out there."

"We've been over this a hundred times, Linc. He *is* better off without me. Right now, he is," I defend when Linc looks to argue with me.

"Ah. And there it is. 'Right now.'"

"I admit it. I hope one day we'll be back together, but if he finds someone before that day, I will be happy for him. I truly will. All I want is for him to be happy," I tell him truthfully.

"What about you?"

"What about me?"

"Don't you deserve that kind of happiness?" he asks.

"I'm not *ready* for that kind of happiness, Lincoln. I am a walking, talking disaster. I need to work on me before there can be a 'we.'" I laugh. "See what I did there?"

One side of his lip lifts. "What if it's too late, then?"

I shrug a shoulder. "Then I find my other someone, too."

"They'll never be him."

"Well, no. No one will ever be him," I whisper.

"Are you really okay with this Dante guy? You trust him?" my protective big brother asks.

"I trust him. He's been nothing but kind."

"He wants to get you in his bed tonight. You ready for that?"

"You're doing 'girl talk' with me? That's usually reserved for Shea."

He nods. "Damn right. I'm very confident in my masculinity."

"With arms bigger than my thighs, I can see why," I tease.

"Stop deflecting."

"I hate that you know me so well."

"Twin curse," he grins.

I sigh. "Yes. I am ready for that. It's been leading up to this and, if I'm being completely honest during this 'girl talk', I'll admit I want to know if I can feel anything other than empty."

"With anyone who *isn't* Xander."

"Yeah."

He pulls me in for a hug. "I get it. I know why you're doing it. I know you're just wasting time until you get back to where you're supposed to be, but I'm gonna step back, Tera. I'm going to let you make these decisions and mistakes and I really fucking hope you learn from them—sooner rather than later."

"Who knows? I might fall in love with Dante," I question, leaning back and looking at him.

"If you haven't already fallen for that slick dude, you're not gonna."

I shove his shoulder, which doesn't budge. "Whatever. I'm gonna get laid tonight."

"I got laid last weekend," he taunts.

"Bravo. Now, it's my turn," I tell him and head downstairs.

There's candlelight, soft music playing in the background, and the handsome man that is Dante DiMora—all waiting for me. Not just for dinner.

"This is beautiful, Dante." It's so much more than that. Roses. There are roses and rose petals scattered about.

I'm not going to lie. I'm nervous. Since the attack, it's only been Xander and that was just one weekend. No one's touched me since... not intimately. I don't know what to expect from Dante or myself.

"Sparkling cider?" he asks.

I nod and take the champagne flute from him. He knows I can't drink alcohol while on the medications I'm on. I appreciate the effort he made to accommodate that. Not every man would.

"Thank you."

He smiles softly. "You are nervous?"

"A little."

He reaches out to rest his hands on my shoulders, pulling me in for a hug. "There is no need, little dove. You know me. I know you."

I nod and inhale his scent. It's an expensive cologne but it definitely does the trick. I feel the tingle of arousal all from his scent—even more so when he leans down to press a soft kiss to the side of my neck.

He kisses my neck, my cheeks, my lips; and when he begins to remove my clothes, his lips touch every part of my body. I knew he was experienced, but I had no idea he'd be a considerate and attentive lover. Every breath, every moan, he learns from, enhancing my pleasure until I come apart in his arms. I'm shaky and wobbly. He carries me to the bed.

I watch as he undresses, removing his tie, shirt, shoes, socks, and slacks, leaving him in black silk boxers. That would seem silly—wasting silk on boxers—if I didn't know him as well as I do. Everything has to be the best for Dante.

Dante winks at me then wiggles his eyebrows as he removes his boxers and I have to laugh.

I look at him naked and he definitely is a sexy man and I want him. He's not as "big" as Xander, but he's definitely not lacking in the endowment department.

No. There is no room for Xander in this bed. I'm positive he doesn't think of me while he fucks other women. I refuse to let him interfere tonight.

I hold out my hand to Dante and he takes it, sliding next to me on the bed. He reaches into the nightstand and pulls out a stream of condoms.

"Whoa. You're definitely prepared," I tease.

He grins. "You think you can handle it?"

"I don't think you can handle *me*," I taunt.

He smirks and dips his fingers between my legs.

"Ah, still so wet and ready for me. It was a beautiful thing to watch you come. I want to see that again."

He rips open the condom and rolls it on.

I pull him down to me. The feel of his fingers rubbing me ignited the spark again.

Slowly, he positions himself at my entrance.

"Are you sure?" he asks, one last time.

I nod. "I am."

With that, he gently slips inside me. Inch by inch, watching my face as he does, gauging my expression. His eyes darken and glaze over, and when he's fully inside of me, he groans.

"You feel amazing."

I'm dying here. He's going so slow and I want hard and dirty. I don't want slow. I don't want sweet. I want him to fuck me. I want to come. I want to know I can feel that with someone other than—

"Please," I beg.

"What do you want, darling?"

"I need you to move."

So he does, but it's slow again, and I'm frustrated.

"Dante," I say as I reach up to hold his face in my hands.

"Mmm," he replies.

"Faster. I want it fast."

"You want me to fuck you?" he probes with a devilish grin as he continues his slow but deep thrusts—driving me insane.

"Yes. I *need* you to fuck me hard," I mewl, all but begging.

He winks at me. "You only need to tell me and I will give you anything you want."

He lifts one of my legs over his hip and begins a hard, steady rhythm. He gets so deep and it feels so good, I lift the other leg and lock them behind his back, arching my back, lifting my hips to meet him in the middle.

"Oh, yes," I moan when he thrusts hard and begins moving faster. "Just like that, please…"

Nonsensical things fly from my mouth, begging, pleading for him to give me the orgasm I'm chasing but is just out of reach.

"Not yet. It's too good and I don't want it to end yet."

"Dante…"

We move and moan and sweat and pant and fuck like it's the last time we'll ever be able to fuck anyone again. It's a hard, pounding rhythm now, one that sends the sparks to a steady, increasing burn.

"Oh, God. Please," I beg.

"You're so wet and hot—so tight. Mmm, Tera you're magnificent."

"I need to come, Dante. Please make me come."

He doesn't hesitate. He shifts us, just a little, but it's everything. It gives me what I couldn't get…

"Oh yes, yes, yes," I cry out as the orgasm nears.

He leans down and sucks on my nipple, then bites the tip gently between his teeth. That's it. I explode, like, major detonation.

"Yes!" I moan as the orgasm barrels through me, wicked and hot and sharp, almost painful.

He groans over me, his body shuddering, his breath stuttering out as he comes.

I can't watch him come. I don't know why. I just can't.

When he stills, he rolls us to our side, giving this an air of intimacy I don't want to experience. I lean back, lift my hands to push my hair out of my face, looking everywhere but at him. I know he knows what I'm doing. I know he's watching me. I just don't know what to do next.

He fixes that problem for me. He slips out of me and out of the bed toward the bathroom. "I'll be right back."

I merely nod as I roll to my back, slipping under the covers and pulling them up to my chest. I stare at the ceiling.

I can't believe I just slept with someone who isn't Xander. I close my eyes and fight back the tears, but they slip out anyway. I can't stop them no matter how hard I try, so I give up and let them fall.

Dante must have anticipated this because, when he comes back from the bathroom, he's carrying a box of tissues. He pulls a couple free and hands them to me, taking one for himself to wipe my tear-stained cheeks.

"Come here, darling," he says softly, kindly, as he sits with his back against the headboard. He pulls me onto his lap, nearly cradling me, letting me purge the grief, the pain, the ache, the shame.

He whispers sweet words and holds me while I cry.

"I-I'm sorry," I sob.

"Hush. Don't you dare apologize for being human," he replies.

I hate that I'm doing this after we just had sex. I don't want him to think it's about him. This has everything to do with me and the fact I gave myself to someone other than my estranged husband—the love of my life, the one I forced out of my life.

Finally, the tears let up and I look at Dante, my makeup likely smeared everywhere.

"I don't want you to think I'm crying because of you or what we just did. It's not."

"Shh," he whispers, taking a tissue and wiping beneath my eyes. "I know, Tera. I know you. I know your heart. So, I know what the tears are about."

"I did this," I sniffle. "I told him to go. I want him to be happy."

"Darling, what makes you think he wasn't happy with you?" Dante asks, sliding us down so we're lying face-to-face, hands held as if we're about to arm wrestle.

"The photos. The fact that he couldn't live the rockstar life—not completely, like the others are. It's unfair for him. He deserves to experience all of that. The groupies, the parties, the other musicians, the fame, the fortune, and the sex. That's what the rocker life is all about, right? Sex, drugs, and rock and roll—especially to those who are young like Xander is," I confess.

"Did you talk to him about this?" Dante asks patiently.

"I have. Multiple times."

"And?"

"And he always gives me the same answer—the one he knows I need to hear. After everything that we've been through, after the distance between us physically, emotionally, and geographically, I don't know if he's still being honest with himself."

"You think he'd want to live the life his friends are, but he wouldn't want to tell you because it would hurt you?"

I nod.

"I want more for him. I want him to have everything, to experience everything, as a true rockstar should. They made it to number one and they let themselves, for just one night, enjoy themselves. They didn't have to think about the media. They didn't have to worry about *me*. They shouldn't have to," I admit.

"But—"

"Ben was right, Dante. I heard him ask why it was wrong for them to be able to enjoy one night. They worked so hard for this. They *earned* the right to party however they want to party and without restrictions. Their security, their crew—they all deserved that night. And, because of me, they woke up in a panic when they saw the images. That memory, the one of them hitting number one for the first time, will forever be tainted because of their obligation to me. I don't want that for them and I sure as hell don't want to be an obligation to anyone."

"I can understand that, Tera. But what I'm hearing here is you talking about what everyone else deserves. What about you? What do you deserve? Don't you deserve for your husband and family to respect you enough to not have you humiliated in the press? Don't you deserve the happiness and peace I know you find with Xander?"

"No. Not right now," I admit.

"Why not, Darling?"

"I need to figure out who I am before I can deserve any of that, before I have the right to demand it. I need to know if I'm still the girl who loves Xander as I once did. I need to know I want to step into that spotlight with him one day. I need to know that one day, I'll be strong enough to do that very thing, but right now, I'm not. I don't deserve him. I don't deserve his sacrifice if I can't make one for him, too," I say aloud, realizing the real reason I let Xander go.

"So, is that it then? For you and Xander?" Dante asks me softly.

"For now. I need to be who he fell in love with and I need to be strong enough to face the chaos that goes with his lifestyle. I'm neither of those."

"You're so much stronger than you think."

"Not really. I'm pretty much a coward. It'd be different if I knew without a doubt nothing like the attack would happen to me again, but no one knows that. That fear paralyzes me, Dante. It terrifies me to feel someone's eyes on me, to have anyone standing behind me, to feel a stranger's breath on the back of my neck."

He looks at me questioningly.

"One night in the gallery, I was helping Angelina set up for a show. One of the workers asked me if the painting was straight. I could see a slant to the left. He meant no harm, only to see what I saw, so he stood behind me to get that perspective. I *knew* I was safe. I knew he wasn't going to hurt me, but I flashed back to that night when I was on my stomach and his alcohol-drenched breath filled my nostrils—well, that and the metallic scent of my blood," I hiccup, recovering from my ugly cry.

"Jesus, Tera." He pulls me close. "Did you talk to someone about this?"

I nod. "I have sessions with my therapist once a week. We had an emergency session when I walked blindly up the stairs to my apartment and Lincoln found me in the middle of the kitchen, in the dark, vomiting into the trash can."

"I see. You don't have to help with the gallery, Tera. You know that, don't you? We don't expect that from you," he tells me.

"I do. I know that, but I enjoy it and it's the only place I can go without stepping outside. I need that."

"But you don't need the added trauma."

"No, but how will I know what my triggers are if I never experience them?" I wonder aloud.

He kisses my forehead. "Are you hungry?"

"I could eat."

"Then let's eat and, if you're up for it, we can come back to bed. We can just sleep if that's what you want. We can fuck if you want that. Or, if you need space, I'll walk you up to your apartment and say goodnight like a true gentleman," he states.

"You're such a good man, Dante. Why would you want to waste your time with a train wreck like me?"

"You're truly lovely and you're wild between the sheets."

I laugh, as does he.

"Let's eat and go from there," I offer.

He nods, pulls on his boxers, and hands me his five-hundred-dollar button-down shirt to wear.

"So," I say as we head to the kitchen, "what've you got to eat?"

Chapter Seven

Xander

THERE'S A SMOKIN' hot chick hanging all over me but I pay her no attention. I'm too busy looking at the image of Tera with *Dante* at her latest show. That fucker. I knew he wanted her. Who wouldn't? But the fact that he's made a move pisses me off like nothing else.

"What's got you looking like you want to kill someone?" Ethan asks.

I show him, and he winces and nods. "Yeah, I saw that."

"You knew, huh?"

He nods again.

"How long?"

"It's not serious," he hedges.

"How long?" I ask again.

"A couple weeks. They're just..." He trails off, looking extremely uncomfortable.

"They're just fucking," Jesse says bluntly.

"How the fuck do you know?" I bite out. If he knew and didn't tell me...

"Dude, it's obvious she's not invested. His arm is around her. Hers are nowhere near him," he reasons. "And, no. I didn't know. I just found out right now when you did."

"Tera doesn't just 'fuck'. She's gotta feel something for him if she's sleeping with him."

Ethan sighs. "Okay. Here's what I know. They went on a couple of dates, they're fucking, but they're not exclusive."

I raise my brows.

"I asked Lincoln, alright? I knew you'd want to know eventually," Ethan replies.

"Thanks, man."

"Who is she?" the chick hanging on me asks.

"None of your fucking business is who she is," I tell her.

"Rude," she whines.

"Don't like it? Move the fuck along."

She huffs and walks away. Her spot is replaced with a busty blonde within seconds.

I have no time to baby these chicks. I don't want to. They're nothing to me. Just an easy piece of ass.

Jesse chuckles and raises his beer in a toast. He doesn't put up with their shit either. They get what they want. They get to fuck a rockstar and brag about it to their friends.

"Put the phone away, man," Jesse demands. "Let's get the hell out of here and go back to the hotel. I've got a little something planned."

The chick next to me claps and Jesse gives her a look.

"You're not invited," he informs her.

The girl next to him snorts. The one next to me stiffens.

"Likely, you're not invited either," she tells the chick with Jesse.

"She's invited," is all Jesse says. The other chick starts swearing and security pulls her out of the room.

"Dude," I say with a laugh.

"Come on, Xan," the chick with Jesse says. "Let's go have some fun."

I lift a brow at Jesse and he just winks. Well, okay then.

We get back to the room and the minute the door closes, the chick grabs me and pulls me in for a kiss. I turn my head.

"No. I don't do kissing," I tell her. "Not on the mouth anyway."

She snickers. "I'm Dani, by the way."

I nod. She makes her way into the bedroom and I look at Jesse.

"What's the plan?"

"Threesome, dude. This chick is a lot to handle and I didn't think you'd mind helping out," he answers.

"Not exactly what comes to mind when I think 'threesome', but I'm game."

"We won't do anything too crazy."

I nod and look at Jesse. I trust him. He trusts me.

"You do this before?"

"First time," he tells me.

"Same."

"Then let's make it count."

She's already naked when we get into the room.

"Dude," I whisper. "I don't go down on strange chicks.

Especially ones who are as easy as this one."

"Fuck no. She may be one of my regular chicks, but I don't know where she's been. So just finger her a bit, suck her tits, fuck her, but there won't be any pussy licking," he assures me. "You up for this?"

I nod. "Why wouldn't I be?"

"The Tera thing."

"This isn't the first chick I've fucked since Tera and I called it quits and she damn sure won't be the last."

"What about the fact that you're not even a little bit hard?" he asks, cupping me through my jeans.

"Dude…" I trail off, feeling my cock getting hard from just the feel of his hand over my pants.

"There's bound to be some overlap," Jesse tells me. "I wouldn't trust anyone else, man. I'm not into you like that."

"Good, 'cause I'm not like that, Jesse. No matter who it is. This won't blur any lines?" I ask.

"Nah. Sex is sex. What happens in this room stays in this room."

I meet his gaze and nod. Just that simply, everything's cool. No weirdness, no fucked up feelings.

We make our way to the bed, undressing as we go.

"I'm not gonna hang out too long," I inform them both.

"But you're gonna stay long enough to fuck me, right?" Dani asks.

"Damn straight. Play with your pussy so you're wet before we even get there," I command. She does and it's hot. She's shaved, which is okay, I guess, but completely bare reminds me of little girls and that's fucking sick, dude. I prefer a woman who trims. That's fucking sexy as hell. Maybe I only think that because that's what Tera does.

Tera. I can't believe she's fucking that guy.

Jesse reaches down and replaces Dani's finger with his own.

"Is she wet?" I ask.

He looks up and smirks. "Oh yeah."

While he handles the business below, I lean in to suck on her nipples a bit. She's got a really great rack. No fake tits for this one. Natural and... oh hell. I lose my train of thought when she wraps her hand around my cock and starts stroking. I look over and she's doing the same to Jesse while he teases her pussy.

"Stop teasing me," she tells him and Jesse chuckles.

"Greedy."

"Damn right. Women can have multiple orgasms so let's see if you can give 'em to me, boys," she says in a fake southern drawl.

I snort. "She doubts us, man."

Jesse nods. "I know it. She doesn't know what she's asking for."

"Give her one. Just a taste. I expect you to keep a running tally."

Within seconds, she's moaning in ecstasy as Jesse finger fucks her while rubbing her clit.

"How do you want to do this?" I ask Jesse.

"She got her first orgasm, so it's our turn. You fuck her while she sucks me off."

She moans. "I don't know how much of you I can fit in my mouth, Jesse."

"Just take as much as you can," he replies, moving to stand next to her. She needs no encouragement. She grabs his cock and starts sucking on it like a pro.

I roll a condom on my cock and slide up between her legs on the bed. I lift her legs over mine, tilting her hips up before I push inside her.

"How does she feel?" Jesse asks.

"Tight. Hot. Wet," I tell him as I start fucking her. I start out slowly, enjoying the feel of her pussy surrounding me.

"She's good," Jesse tells me with a groan.

"I can see that. You're not gonna last, dude."

"Hell yeah, I am. Feels too good to blow this fast."

"Yeah," I agree, starting to fuck her faster, and Jesse reaches down to start tweaking her nipples. Each time he pinches one, her pussy clenches around my cock and I groan. Jesse chuckles. "Not fair."

"Are you complaining?"

"Fuck no."

She doubles her efforts with Jesse, taking more of his cock into her mouth. I don't know how she does it. Jesse's gotta be a good ten inches.

"Shit," I curse, feeling the tingling beginning at the base of my spine, my cock swelling as I get close to coming.

"Take her hard, man. A little something to remember you by."

"I don't wanna come until she does. She's getting close again."

"Go ahead. I'll help you out." He teases and pinches her nipples and I grab her hips and start pounding into her.

She's close. So close... and so am I.

I close my eyes and picture Tera—before all of this bullshit happened, when she had love and light in her eyes. When she loved me. When she wanted me. When I made love to her for the first time after the attack. When she gave herself to me—all of herself.

I can only hear Tera in my head as she cried out in surprise when she came, the look on her face as she did. The feel of her pussy clenching so fucking tight around me. Jesus.

I'm not even sorry that I blow before this chick does, but it's not long before she joins, making my orgasm feel even that much better.

I let out one last groan, then bow my head, eyes closed.

I wish this was you, baby. I wish...

I pull out and toss the condom.

"You outta here?" Jesse asks knowingly.

"Yeah, man."

He gives me a look and I know it's one that says he's sorry about Tera. But it's not his place to be sorry. What's done is done.

I walk out of the room, feeling hollow and empty, the same as I've felt for the last six months without her.

The word *settled* flows through my mind and all I can think in reply is: *Fuck you.*

I'm not ready yet. If I'm not ready, she sure as hell isn't. So we stay apart.

For now.

Chapter Eight

Tera

DANTE AND I have been casually seeing one another the last four months. We have a no-strings arrangement—meaning, when he goes out of town to his other galleries, he's free to fuck whoever he wants.

The same goes for me... and I have. I've fucked a couple of guys who are regular patrons at the gallery. One was a mind-blowing quickie in the gallery restroom—he's been back a couple of times. Then, there's Clark—that experience was horrifying. From the way he fumbled, I was worried he was a virgin... so I left him alone in the bathroom. That's too much work for a quick orgasm.

Now, Carter Winters walks into my gallery showing and I can't believe my eyes.

"Tera!" he shouts across the room, heads turning in our direction as he strides quickly to me, pulling me up into his arms, spinning and hugging me tightly. I can feel those eyes on me and it raises the hairs on the back of my neck. Then I sink into the warmth that is Carter and remember I'm safe.

"Carter!" I laugh. He sets me down. "What are you doing here?"

"I heard you were having a show and I felt like a dick for never coming before now," he admits.

"You're not a dick. You've been busy with football and school. Dude, you're being drafted into the NFL your junior year of college! I am so happy for you!" I hug him again.

"Yeah? I'm pretty stoked. It's all happening so fast. But I'm gonna do it right. I'm gonna finish my degree with tutors—just in case, ya know?" he says with that cute tilt of his head.

I smile. I can't stop smiling. "I always knew you were smarter than you looked."

"Hey!" he laughs.

I shake my head. "I am *so* happy to see you. I've missed you. You used to come over more."

He hangs his head sheepishly. "I know. I'm sorry. I just can't keep up with all the demands on my awesomeness."

I laugh out loud, really loud, then snort. Heads swivel in our direction again and I don't even care. I keep grinning. A flash goes off, then another. I freeze and grit my teeth. I'm not a stranger to the occasional photos from the press at my showings, but this is a private moment. This is what I don't want, why I need to stay out of the Falling Down spotlight. I'm not strong enough for it. Not right now.

"Ah, they've spotted you," I inform him with a forced smile.

"Let's pose," he proposes with a wink.

In true Carter Winters fashion, he doesn't wait for my response. He merely wraps an arm around my waist, so I do the same to him. I lean into his side and he looks down at me. Shutters are clicking right and left as I turn to look up at him. He's safety. His smile is infectious and it isn't long before we're both laughing. This is the freest I've felt in such a long time.

He hugs me close and I hug him back, closing my eyes and inhaling his familiar spicy scent.

"You still fit, doll face," he says as we pull apart.

I nod. "You always were a good hugger."

"I'm good at more than just that," he teases, wiggling his eyebrows.

"Oh, I remember."

Angelina walks over. With Dante out of the country, Angelina flew in from the LA gallery to help me with my show. "I have someone interested in the bridge piece. Do you have a moment?"

I nod. "If you'll excuse me?"

"Heck no," Carter answers. "I'm coming along. I want to see the professional in action."

"Whatever works for you," I say with a grin.

I'm explaining what the piece symbolizes and answering the potential buyer's questions when Carter begins to wander, stopping at each piece of my work to examine them. I'm distracted now, as he nears a painting I don't want him to see. He'll recognize the trauma, the symbolism in the image even as the most astute art connoisseur only skims over it.

I hurry the buyer, hating that I am, but hating the stiff set to Carter's shoulders as he approaches the image I'd hoped he wouldn't see.

"I'll take it," Mr. Zonberg tells Angelina, and I smile brightly, thanking him profusely before excusing myself.

I don't say anything. I merely stand beside Carter as he stares blankly at the scene before him. It's a scene I still see vividly in my head.

"This…" he begins, then swallows thickly.

"Carter. I'd hoped you'd skip this one."

He shakes his head, not looking away from the dark painting. "I can't. It's exactly what I saw when I… heard."

I reach over and thread my fingers with his, squeezing his hand a bit. We've never discussed what he went through, and yet I know it was a majorly traumatic incident for him. He needed extensive therapy, but even I know therapy can't rid a person of the memories.

"I wish you'd hung up," I whisper, watching his face.

"What? How could I? I couldn't leave you alone, Tera. I just… you needed me," he says, voice cracking.

I tug his hand and he looks down at me, this big amazing man who was just a boy then.

"Thank you."

He nods. "You know I'd do anything for you."

"I know." I reach up to touch his cheek and he leans into my hand. He's got a few days' worth of stubble on his face and it tickles my thumb as I rub it across his cheek.

He pulls me close, into a hug, and I hold him tight. My body begins to shake from the memory and from the knowledge that everything that was done to me, he experienced, too.

"Are… are you okay, now?" he asks, not letting go.

I shake my head. "No. I don't go outside and, if you'll notice, the crowd is very thin in here. I don't handle larger groups of people well. Even for this I needed anti-anxiety medication."

He nods, his cheek resting on top of my head now.

People begin murmuring about us, staring, more flashes going off. Angelina comes over.

"The last of the pieces sold, Tera. You're free to leave, if you wish." Her expression is one of concern. All the pieces but this one. This one isn't for sale.

"Thank you, Angelina. You're a godsend. I wouldn't make it through these things without you," I respond honestly.

"You and your talent—you make it easy." She gives me a small smile and walks away.

I turn to Carter, who looks so lost. "C'mon. Let's go up."

He doesn't say anything, just follows along blindly as I lead him up the stairs to the apartment. I close and lock the door with the keypad and the reinforced chain, knowing no one is expected to come up.

"It's quiet up here," he murmurs, still holding my hand like a lifeline.

"Yeah. Linc's out of town until tomorrow."

"He still lives with you, then?"

I nod. "Want something to drink? Beer? Tea? Soda?"

"Tea, if it's not too much trouble."

"No trouble at all. With just a half-teaspoon of sugar, right?" I ask.

He nods. "Perfect."

"Make yourself comfortable," I urge.

Carter wanders the apartment aimlessly, stopping to look at the photographs—laughing at the one with us sticking our tongues out at one another and crossing our eyes. We were so silly back then. Silly and carefree. Right now, he looks like the weight of the world just fell on his shoulders—and I hate that it's because of what happened to me.

I bring the tea in the living room and we both sit on the sofa, the only light coming from the kitchen, leaving the room dim and calming.

"What's going on in there, Carter?" I ask quietly.

He sighs and tips his head back, staring at the ceiling. "That night… I didn't know what was going on, at first. I only knew you were in trouble. I immediately went to my dad and he called 911. The cops tracked your phone and, Jesus, they didn't make it in time."

He scrubs his hands over his face, then leans forward to grab his tea before resting his elbows on his knees.

"I knew what they were doing, too, Tera. They laughed and joked about it, so I knew. I was paralyzed in fear for you. I didn't know if they were just going to hurt you or if they were going to kill you. One of them mentioned a gun. Another mentioned a switchblade. I sat in a corner in the hallway while my dad frantically spoke to the police. He kept reassuring me it would be okay, but I knew it wouldn't. Nothing was okay."

I stay silent so he can continue to purge anything he needs to. Hearing this from him isn't an easy thing for me. It's tearing me in half again. He mentions something they said or did and I feel it, I hear it.

"You stopped talking. I thought you were dead. I couldn't stand it, but then something even worse happened. You started mewling out this awful sound of distress, and you screamed in pain. It sounded like an animal being abused, but I knew it was you. That, to me, was worse than death. Hearing you suffer like that…" He pauses, wiping the tears from his eyes then taking a drink of his tea.

He leans back against the sofa again, turning his head to look at me.

"I was still in love with you, and hearing you hurt, hearing them hurt you, it was as if they were delivering the punishment directly to my heart. Then you went silent again and I didn't know what happened—if they killed you, or if you just… broke. Eventually, I knew you were alive. They talked about how it was pissing them off to *not* hear your crying, even though you *were* crying. They wanted to hear you suffer. Seeing it wasn't enough."

I nod and wipe my own tears, my body beginning to shake. Carter reaches out and cups my cheek.

"I wanted to kill someone that night. I would have killed them all if I'd been able to get there in time. It felt like hours, I'm sure it did to you, too. In actuality, it was only like twenty minutes or something—if that."

"They did maximum damage in minimal time," I whisper hoarsely, my voice cracking.

Carter sets his mug down on the table, doing the same with mine, before pulling me onto his lap and holding me tight. I know this is more for him than me. Whatever he needs...

"Then they were gone. It was a few minutes before I heard you whimpering. I was going crazy being in Chicago when you needed me in LA. I knew I should have gone along on that trip. Something told me I needed to go but I didn't listen. I mean, you had Xander. I thought he'd have been there," he tells me desperately.

"But he wasn't," I whisper.

"No. He wasn't. You were alone because you took the time to talk to him without distraction before you left. You sacrificed so much for him at that time, what with the band and touring," he reminds me.

"I did. I didn't mind. Not until that night," I reply.

"Do you—" He shakes his head.

"Go ahead and ask. It's okay."

He gives me an uncertain look. "Do you... did you ever blame him?"

I nod. "Oh yeah. It's only natural. I mean, like you said, I stayed late and alone for him. If I hadn't, none of that would have happened. If he'd been there for my big night, like I'd been for him countless times, none of it would have happened."

"I blamed him."

I look at him in surprise.

"I did. I still do. If he'd fucking been there… if he'd just *once* put you first, you wouldn't have been attacked," Carter bites out with anger.

I nod. "I know. I thought that so much, but can I blame him, really? I was the one who wanted to talk to him without interruptions, so I stayed at the gallery alone. I could have talked to him on speaker in the car, but I didn't want to have to deal with traffic and talk at the same time."

"Are you really blaming yourself for this?" he asks, clearly pissed.

"No. God, no. I never blamed myself, but all the 'what ifs' went through my mind while I recovered in the hospital. I spent a lot of time sedated, and all a person does then is sleep or think. I didn't want to talk to anyone so I pretended to be asleep even when I wasn't. I didn't want to see them. They could be there for this but not for the biggest night of my life? You see, I've thought it all. I've told them all every one of my thoughts. It's part of therapy," I tell him.

He nods. "When I saw you…" He clears his throat. "When I saw you lying in that bed, I didn't know if death would have been better. That's a fucked up thing to think. I know that now, but then, you were so broken and lost. I'm glad you didn't die, Tera, but I am so fucking sorry you had to go through all of that."

I wipe his tears. "I know, but don't you be sorry. You *saved* my life, Carter. There's no way anyone would have found me in that alley. It was dark. I would have likely bled to death."

He hugs me tighter and I hug him back.

"I wish I could have done more. I've never felt so fucking helpless in my life and I never want to feel that way again," he admits.

I nod against his cheek. I don't know how long we sit like that, just holding one another while we purge the grief. All I know is, we both needed this.

"What the holy fucking hell is going on here?" Lincoln bellows.

I blink my eyes open and meet Carter's amused ones. We must have fallen asleep. Carter arranged us so we were lying face to face and he covered us, too.

I wink at him and he smirks.

"Oh, Carter, right there," I moan, with a sassy grin.

He grunts for effect, trying like hell to not laugh.

"God damn, Tera," Lincoln chides.

I let the laugh loose and so does Carter.

"That was awesome," Carter declares.

"I'm not amused," Linc replies.

"I don't care," I tell Lincoln with a snicker as we sit up—still fully clothed. "As you can see by the lack of nudity, no funny business went on here last night."

"I see that now, but the photos of you and Carter at your show last night look like something entirely different," Linc tells me, handing me his phone.

"Ah, the press," I murmur.

Carter whistles at some of the intimate-looking images that have hit the Internet. "We look hot, like we're gonna rip each other's clothes off right there."

I laugh. "We do. Sadly, it was quite the opposite."

"Sadly?" Linc questions.

I shrug. "If I'm going to be accused of banging Carter Winters, I'd really like to do it so I can enjoy all the pleasures I know he can deliver."

Lincoln groans. "More than I needed to know."

Carter laughs. "Coffee?"

"Cabinet on the right by the fridge," I tell him.

He nods and heads to the kitchen. With the open concept of this apartment, there isn't much privacy when Linc gives me a look.

"What?"

"Your husband is pissed."

I laugh. "Are you serious right now?"

"As a heart attack. You know Winters is a hot topic for Xan."

"That's his problem. Whores and groupies are a hot topic for me, but that didn't seem to stop him from being photographed on a regular basis, and it certainly didn't stop him from making a sex tape of a threesome with Jesse and one of their sluts, now, did it?" I bite back.

"Don't shoot the messenger. I'm just saying."

"I know what you're saying and I don't give a shit. He didn't care that I had to see all the disgusting images and gossip after that sex tape hit the airwaves, did he? Nope, sure didn't. So I don't give one single fuck how he feels about this."

Lincoln nods. "I hate this shit. You two need to figure this shit out."

"I thought we already had."

He points at me and raises his brows. "You know better than that."

"Whatever," I reply when Carter hands me a cup of steaming coffee.

"I think it's fantastic. It's about time that asshole gets a taste of his own medicine," Carter tells us with a grin.

"Yeah!" I agree. "What Carter said."

Linc rolls his eyes. "It's like high school all over again."

I laugh.

"Not funny, little sister."

"It is for me," I tease.

"Yeah, yeah. You're not stuck in the middle—again."

Carter cocks his head. "Again? You mean, he was like this back then, too?"

Linc nods.

"I thought it was one-sided," Carter mutters. "I should have known." He pauses. "What a fucking idiot! Again!"

Lincoln nods and points at Carter. "Exactly, and she's no better."

Carter looks at me thoughtfully.

"What?"

"Why?" he asks.

"Why what?"

"Why are you wasting time, Tera? You know as well as I do it can all end in a split second," Carter questions.

I sigh. "I can't be what he needs me to be."

"And what's that, exactly?"

"His wife. Standing next to him in the spotlight. I can't do that. I can't even step outside of this building without panicking so bad I hyperventilate," I admit quietly.

"You're still in therapy, right?" Carter asks.

I nod. "I'm working on it. I'm just not there yet."

"Ah. So you're not wasting time. You're using it to heal and get strong again. I get it."

I wrap my arms around his neck and hug him.

"Finally," I whisper. "Someone understands."

"You're really not that complicated," Carter mutters.

"You keep right on thinking that, pal." With that, Lincoln walks out of the room with luggage in tow.

Carter gives me an amused smile. "You giving your brother a hard time?"

I shrug. "Isn't that what sisters are supposed to do?"

Carter chuckles. "It's what mine does. I didn't know you could be so evil."

I wiggle my eyebrows. "What you don't know won't hurt you."

"Truth. I can live without knowing."

I nod and take another sip of coffee.

"Thanks for last night," Carter voices quietly.

"Thank you, too. We both needed to talk it through. I hate so much that you suffered as much as I did," I whisper.

"I'll admit I suffered, but nowhere near as much as you, baby doll. You went through something too horrible to put into words. They broke you, yet here you are, putting the pieces back where they belong. I admire the hell out of you, Tera."

I shake my head. "Don't admire me. It's been a constant battle and a lot of the time I think I'm losing."

"You're not. You're winning. Some of those cracks are going to take time to heal and reinforce, but I have absolutely no doubt you'll get there. When you do, I'll be there to help you celebrate."

"Promise?" I ask.

"I promise," Carter answers.

I hug him again. "I'll hold you to that."

Chapter Nine

Nine months later...
(Four Years Before Lucy)

Xander

"I T'S BEEN OVER two years. We missed our five-year anniversary. I can't take this shit anymore," I tell the guys, pacing out on the patio where we're drinking some beer and relaxing after having just finished a long-ass tour.

"What're you gonna do?" Kennedy asks.

"I don't know, but I can't stand being without her."

"Dude, I don't know what's taken you this long," Ben says. "Get your ass out there and fix your shit."

"What the hell are you waiting for?" Jesse asks.

"A written invitation, I think," Ethan adds.

"If that's all it would've taken, I'd have sent one a long time ago," Kennedy declares.

"Funny fuckers. All of you. We were touring, in case you forgot. It's not so easy knocking on her door when we're touring Europe and the UK." I pace some more. "You all think you know so much, tell me. How the hell do I fix this?"

Kennedy leans forward. "You might wanna start by... "

Chapter Ten

Tera

I'M DEEP INTO my work when there's a knock on the door. *Which one of them is it?* With the way things are set up, the only ones who can get through this level of security are the people on the list.

I wipe my hands on the paint rag and look through the peep-hole. My heart plunges into my stomach.

"Holy shit. Holy fucking shit," I whisper. I turn around and pace. What's he doing here? I don't want to see him, not when a year ago a sex tape of him and Jesse and some slut was released. That was one hell of a threesome.

Yeah, I tortured myself and watched it. It made me really glad I never went public about Xander and me. Watching him parading a different chick around before the cameras every night was one thing, but a sex tape took it to a whole new level. I wanted to file for divorce or legal separation, but somehow Lincoln talked me out of it.

He pounds on the door again and I press a hand to my stomach to try and calm my nerves.

God, why did he have to come now, of all times? I'm painting. My hair's up in a messy bun, I'm covered in paint, and I'm makeup-less. Plus, I've been working nonstop on this piece, so I'm plagued with dark circles under my eyes from lack of sleep.

Maybe he'll go away.

Ugh.

I unlock the deadbolts and the chain before opening the door. I keep my pissed off in place in spite of how fucking delicious he looks right now. Oh God. I've missed him so much.

I want nothing more than to run my fingers through his messy dark curls, pull his face down, and kiss him stupid. But I don't.

I don't say anything. I just wait with raised eyebrows.

"Tera," he says softly, with such reverence I nearly drop to my knees—nearly.

"Yes?" I ask.

"I brought you a coffee," he replies, holding out a large cardboard cup from my favorite coffee place.

I really want to accept that coffee. I could use it, and I bet it's my favorite. What I really want is to invite Xander in, but instead, I give him an eye roll and close the door, relocking the chain and deadbolts.

I stand there and wait, knowing he's on the other side. I hear a thump, and I can picture him resting his head against the door.

I walk away because if I don't, I'm going to do something stupid and open the door, take the coffee, let him in, share the coffee, then take him to bed—and I can't do that. I won't. I can't.

I think about everything that's happened. I think about his showing up out of the blue. Who the hell does he think he is? The anger inside me explodes.

"How dare he show up here," I mutter to myself as I pace the length of the kitchen. "I mean, the nerve! After that sex tape and no apology," I growl.

"What's going on?" Linc asks, leaning against the doorjamb, arms crossed, feet crossed at the ankles—the perfect image of someone who's very comfortable in their own skin. It seems to be his favorite pose.

"Xander is what's going on."

"Huh?" Linc asks.

"He showed up."

"Here?"

"Yeah."

"Just now?" He turns his head toward the door.

"Yeah!"

"Why?"

"I don't know. I guess to bring me coffee since he had a big cup and offered it to me."

"You didn't take it?" he questions.

"Do you see any cups of coffee around here?" I ask, exasperated.

"Nope. Is that all he wanted?"

"I dunno and I don't care, Linc. Why would he just show up like that?" I wonder aloud.

"Probably because you won't take his phone calls."

I scoff. "He should be used to that by now. I don't want coffee from him. I don't want him to show up on my doorstep out of the blue. I don't want anything but to finish this piece I'm working on."

"What's that Shakespeare quote? 'Methinks the lady doth protest too much.'"

"Bite me, brother. He made a *sex tape!* A threesome with Jesse!

I'm not supposed to be bothered by that?" I rage.

"I never said that but it was months ago, and it's not like you haven't been getting your fair share of ass," he retorts.

"Yeah, but I'm not stupid enough to fuck someone who's going to make a sex tape so they can leak it for a quick buck and the fast track to fame!" I snap.

"Maybe he wants to talk, explain things. Maybe he just wanted to have coffee. Maybe he wanted to see how you're doing."

"What he wants and what he gets are two different things where I'm concerned." I eye him, and he's got that look, the one that tells me he's hiding something.

"What?" he asks.

"What are you keeping from me? You know I can always tell."

"If you want to know, next time he shows up, and you open the door, try *asking him*."

"No."

"What've you got to lose, T? Don't you think it's been long enough? It's been what, over two years, right?"

I nod. "Two years, five months, and twenty-three days."

"But who's counting, right?" he quips.

"It doesn't matter if I'm counting or not. It doesn't matter if I want to open that door and kiss his face off. It doesn't matter, Lincoln, and do you know why?"

He shakes his head. "No."

"Because I'm angry and resentful and so not ready to stand in the Falling Down spotlight he's going to want me to be in. Maybe not now, maybe not next month, or even next year, but he's going to want that and I may never be able to give him that. I may be too broken to give him what he needs and that will hurt him worse than my keeping the door closed," I tell him, wiping tears off my cheeks, likely smearing paint.

He pulls me close. "Tera. You know him. You know *them*. No

one would ever ask you to do something you're not ready for. *Ever.* I'm not sure what his agenda is, why he came by, but I do know that Ethan told me your husband, Xander Thomas Mackenzie is lost without you. They're home from their overseas tour, and he said he needs you more than he needs to breathe. You know that you're his heart, right? That will never change, no matter how hard you push him away or how hard he pushes back. You two are soul mates, and I think you need to start accepting it."

"I don't want to talk to him because, Lincoln, I'm so angry and resentful. I feel like a child, but the feelings are real, and they're rational and just."

"Then you need to get them out. You need to talk to him and them so you can move past where you are right now."

"What's so wrong with where I am right now?" I ask as I grab a paper towel and blow my nose.

"You're stuck. You have nowhere to go. It's the end of the line, baby sister. So it's time to *communicate* what you're feeling and then explain why. Then, you talk it out and get past it. Don't you think it's time to forgive him? And them?" he asks softly.

I sigh. "I want to. I just don't know how."

"You're a smart girl. You'll figure it out."

I sniffle, looking and feeling pathetic. "Will you go get me some chicken from Sal's?"

"Damn, that sounds good right now. The usual?" he asks.

"Yes, please."

"I'll be back in thirty. Come lock up behind me."

He opens the door and looks down. He steps over it, turns, and meets my gaze.

"He left your coffee."

I bend down and pick it up.

"May as well drink it before it gets cold," Linc tells me as he heads down the stairs. I close the door and relock the deadbolts and chain. I sit down in the rocking chair and stare at the coffee in my hands like it's going to hold the answers to all the secrets of the universe.

I take a sip, and it's still hot. I taste the sweetness of caramel and vanilla and begin to cry in earnest.

Coffee as a peace offering? It's just not enough.

The coffee ends, and instead, he brings me bouquets of flowers—each day a different one. I don't take them from him. I do the same as I did with the coffee. I close the door.

I don't want "gifts." I don't know what it is that I *do* want, but it's not this.

Chapter Eleven

Xander

"I DON'T KNOW what to do, dude. She didn't take the coffee. She didn't accept the flowers. How do I get her to talk to me since Kennedy's idea was shit?" I ask Cage. We're on a teleconference, and I can't stay focused enough for this meeting to be productive, so Cage gave up five minutes ago. He was going to hang up, but I need a fresh perspective, so here I am, asking him.

"I don't think she wants 'things', Xander. If I had to guess, I'd say she wants and needs words," Cage replies.

"Words?"

"Yes, words. I'd start with 'I'm sorry' and continue on with 'I love you'," Cage tells me.

"Dude," Jesse says, "that's what you should do. Right there.

That's so Tera."

"That might've been nice to know eleven days ago," I tell Jesse.

"I wonder what she did with those flowers," Ben ponders. "You think she put 'em in the garbage disposal and shredded those fuckers?"

I flinch. I hope not.

"Nah," Kennedy replies. "Tera would never destroy flowers. They're too pretty. I bet she painted them."

"I can see that," Jesse agrees.

"So, apologize and then tell her I love her?" That's all? It doesn't seem like enough.

Ethan sighs. "Just speak from the heart, man."

"Alright. I'll try it."

"Call back tomorrow and let me know if you want me to punch Ethan for you," Ben teases.

"I will."

I hang up and sit in the hotel room I've been living in for almost two weeks now, and I hope like hell I can get through to her. I'll keep trying until I can. I'm not going to accept anything less.

Chapter Twelve

Tera

THERE'S A KNOCK at the door. Same time every day for the last twelve days. Is he not getting tired of me shutting the door in his face? I don't want coffee, and I don't want flowers—even if they're my favorites.

I unlock and open the door, not hiding the fact I'm annoyed. "Yes?"

He stands there and just looks at me.

It's unnerving, so I snap at him. "What? No presents today?"

One side of his mouth lifts in that sexy endearing smirk I love. My heart hammers in my chest, and it's getting more difficult with each day to close the door, but I need to.

He thrusts out a hand, stopping me from closing the door,

startling me. I look at him in surprise.

"I love you."

He says it in a way that leaves no room for doubt. He means what he says. I'm gaping at him when I move to close the door. He nods and starts down the stairs before it's shut.

I lock up and lean back against the door, staring at… nothing.

"Did that just happen?" I whisper.

"It happened," Linc replies, bringing me a cup of coffee.

"Coffee might not be strong enough," I mutter, and he chuckles.

"He's getting to you."

"He caught me off guard. I wasn't expecting that," I admit. Hearing those words falling from his mouth rendered me stupid. It took me back to what it was like to be loved by him—*really* loved by him.

"Mhmm," is all Linc says as he walks out of the room.

He's breaking through the wall, hammering at it bit by bit. What he doesn't realize is, behind the wall isn't just love for him, there's a whole lot of ugly, too.

The next morning, he stands there in faded jeans and the Rolling Stones tee I bought for him. His hair is damp, and he hasn't bothered to shave in a couple of days. That scruffy look. Oh boy.

"I'm sorry. For all of it. I love you, Tera."

My breath catches and tears well. I close the door before they fall.

Lincoln watches me as the tears stream down my cheeks.

"Come here," he coaxes.

He pulls me into a hug, and my heart won't stop beating hard and fast. That hasn't happened in such a long time.

"He isn't going to quit. He *loves* you."

I nod. "I know."

"Stop the madness, T. Just, let him in."

"I want to, but I'm afraid of what it could mean for me if I do."

"What about what it means for you if you don't?" he retorts. "You don't see it, but I do. He's breathing life back into you."

My breath catches. That's what that is. The pounding of my heart. He makes me feel alive. I haven't felt this way since... before I pushed him out of my life.

I drop to my knees, and Lincoln does the same.

"Are you okay?" he asks, worriedly.

I nod. "Yeah. I am." I pause, then meet his gaze. "You know this is going to get ugly before it gets better, right?"

He nods. "I know. I'm here."

I blow out a breath, then inhale deeply.

"I forgot what it was like," I murmur absently.

"What what was like?" Lincoln asks.

"To feel alive."

The next morning, I make sure I look halfway decent before the designated time, only, the knock I'm waiting for doesn't come.

I sit there and wait, picking at my cuticles. I get more coffee and wait some more. I sit on the sofa across from the door, curling up my legs next to me, resting my elbow and coffee cup on the sofa arm.

Lincoln walks in, looks at me, and walks back out.

After forty-five minutes, I take my empty coffee cup to the

kitchen and put it in the dishwasher. I sigh as I head to the bath-room to brush my teeth.

I look at myself in the mirror above the sink and vow not to cry. I waited too long. What did I think would happen? Xander is a man, after all. He's sensitive and, oh God, he loves me, and I closed the door in his face day after day.

I rinse my mouth, unable to look at my stupid self anymore.

"Stupid, stupid, stupid," I curse under my breath.

This time, it's all on me.

I change out of my jeans and into a pair of yoga pants and the matching Rolling Stones tee to the one Xander wore yesterday. I find my red fuzzy socks and put in *How To Lose A Guy In Ten Days*. The fuzzy socks are to make me feel comfortable and secure while the movie is to torture me because of my stupidity.

I will not cry.

I will not cry.

I will not cry.

I keep repeating it as I lie on the sofa, pulling a blanket over myself, and settling in for a long day of self-loathing.

I end up crying five minutes later. I'm full-on ugly crying when Lincoln comes rushing in.

"What's going on?"

"I-I-I s-suck," I wail.

"Shh," he soothes. "You don't suck. Why do you think you do?"

"I waited t-too long, and h-he didn't come. I wanted him to come today. I was going to let him in," I sob. "I was going to…"

"Shh. It's okay."

"It's not. It'll never be okay again because I'm a stupid girl. Stupid, stupid, stupid girl."

"Tera—" he begins, only to be cut off by a knock at the door.

I jerk upright, out of Linc's arms, and run to the door, my hands full of snotty tissues, my face red and splotchy and tear-stained, but I don't care.

I look through the peephole. Oh, thank you, Jesus. Thank you, thank you, thank you.

I hurriedly unlock the deadbolts, the chain getting caught up and wasting time. *Hurry, hurry, hurry. He might leave!*

I swing the door open and there he is. He's on his knees. He reaches out and hugs my legs, crawling forward to get closer.

"I love you, Tera. I'm so fucking sorry. I know everything's a mess right now, I know you want to close the door again, but please. Please don't close the door, Tera. Please don't close the door," he begs, his body shaking with his pleading.

I let out an involuntary cry and drop to my knees.

His eyes widen. "What's wrong? What happened?" he asks, taking in my tear-stained cheeks.

"Y-you d-didn't come. Y-you're late and I th-thought you weren't coming," I confess.

He rests his forehead against mine. "I'll always come for you, Tera. Always. I can't live without you. I can't do it anymore. I can't pretend it's okay. I can't pretend I'm okay."

I nod against his cheek as I hug him tight.

Chapter Thirteen

Tera

"GET IN HERE, man. You don't want to draw attention to yourself," Linc tells Xander as he picks me up and carries me to the sofa. I don't want to let go of Xander and, thankfully, I don't have to for long. He's there, and he's hugging me, and I'm hugging him, and I'm crying, and he's crying, and it's craziness, and it's chaos, but it's what I need. It's Xander. It's *living*.

I don't know how long we stay like that. Minutes? Hours? We just hold each other, too afraid to let go.

He breathes my name, I breathe his.

"I love you so much, Tera."

"I love you, too, Xan, but there's a lot we need to talk about before it's all unicorns and rainbows," I inform him.

He nods. "I know. I just can't seem to let go."

I laugh. "Me neither."

"We could talk like this," he offers.

"Um, that might not be a good idea. I might punch you in the face," I warn.

He shrugs. "Whatever you need to do."

"I don't want to punch you in the face, but you know my temper gets the best of me sometimes."

"I remember."

We pull back at the same time. We both look ravaged.

I hold out the tissue box for him, and he blows his nose. I follow suit.

"I think I'm going to make some tea. My throat is sore. Would you like some? Soda, coffee, beer?"

"Tea's good. Not normally my thing, but yours is always fruity."

I smile at that.

When we're resettled in, I bring some pastries, cookies, chips, and two bottles of water, as well.

"Uh," Xander mutters, looking at me. "Planning on being here a while?"

"There's a lot, Xan. So much more than I ever realized."

He nods.

"I've been seeing my therapist twice a week, and I've talked things through with a couple of my friends," I inform him.

"Good. That's good you could get it out and make sense of things. The guys duct taped my mouth shut a couple of times. Ben threatened to super glue it."

I snicker. "He's so mean."

Xander chuckles. "He *is* mean. The fucker."

I laugh.

"Tell me, Tera. Tell me all of it. If you need to yell, scream, throw shit, punch me—whatever you need, please do it. We can't keep on like this. I can't."

I nod. "Okay." I blow out a breath. "Where to begin?"

"What's weighing on you most? What's the first thing that you think of when you remember your anger?"

"It's not just anger, Xan."

"What do you mean?"

"Let me tell you a story," I tell him about Carter and how I realized I'm not only angry, but I also resent him, them, the band. "I resent the fact that you didn't make it to my big night. I resent the fact that I stayed behind after everyone left so we could talk. That's me accommodating you—again. Then—"

"Stop. You don't have to say it. I know it. I think it every day. If I could go back and redo it, I'd be there. I didn't know how to handle it when I got there, to the hospital and found out everything, and then I realized I could've prevented all of your pain," he admits.

"Not just you, Xander. *All* of you. You all chose the band over me—again. It'd become so second nature that I resigned myself to that fact. I can't do that anymore. I won't. I don't want to resent you. I don't want to be so angry I sometimes think I hate you. I don't. I don't really—hate you, I mean. I just get so—I don't know. I need to come first. I need to know that I do. The darkness is a terrible place for me to be," I admit.

"I get that. So, uh, I saw the photos of you and Carter," he states carefully.

"Yeah? He's such a good guy. We needed to have that talk—he needed it. I'm glad he showed up that night."

Xan nods then takes a sip of his tea. "I don't have the right to ask—"

I laugh humorlessly. "No, you certainly do *not*, sex-tape boy.

Are you fucking kidding me? How stupid are you and Jesse? I expected better from you both."

Xan winces. "Not our finest hour."

I snort. "That's stating the obvious."

"Cage got all the videos down from everywhere. I don't know how, but he did," Xan states.

"Really?"

"Yeah, he's magical, that guy."

"Hmm. Hold on a second." I pick up my phone and dial Shea. "Hey, can you do me a favor and send me the thing we promised never to talk about again?"

"What for? Why would you want to watch that shit again? It wasn't very good anyway. Amateurs," Shea scoffs.

I laugh. "I know, I know. I just need it to prove a point."

Silent pause.

"Oh, snap. He's there, isn't he? Duuuuude. He's in so much trouble! I'll send it now."

"Thanks," I reply, but she already hung up.

A few minutes later an email comes through. I open it, press play, and turn the phone so Xander can see it.

"Fuck," he swears. "How?"

"People can make copies and who knows how many did before Cage got all the copies taken down. How long do you think it'll be before they start popping up all over again?" I ask.

"Fuck. Fuck!"

"Yep."

"Shit, Tera. I'm—"

"Sorry. I know. That doesn't change the fact it's out there. Same with the photos from the big party night. It's all out there, and it's not going away, Xan. You can't expect me to be okay with all of this. You and another chick fucking for the whole world to see? I mean... what the fuck, Xan? After everything that's happened and all of *this,* you can't expect me to step out into your spotlight with you. I'll be humiliated, ridiculed. I can't do that. I won't."

"I know, and I understand, Tera. I really did do a lot of thinking during our time apart."

"When did you have time?" I snark, standing up to begin to pace. "I mean between the concerts, the groupies, the models, the actresses, the *threesomes…* how ever did you find the time to *think*?"

"What about Dante? Carter? Who else was there?" he asks.

"You don't have the right to know. I kept my life as private as I could. You *flaunted* yours. You knew I'd see, but you either didn't care, or you did it on purpose to hurt me. Which was it?" I yell.

"Depended on the day. Some days I wanted you to hurt like I did. Some days I didn't want to think of you at all. It was easier to not think of you. But that didn't work out so well," he admits.

"Yeah. Imagine that. It went both ways, Xan. I didn't purposefully pose with Dante for photos. They were at my shows. I can't control which photos the press chooses to release."

"But you were fucking him."

"I was."

"How long?"

I lift a shoulder. "Six months?"

"Fuck me. Six months. Is it serious?"

"No. It *wasn't.* I'm not seeing him anymore, and I know you don't want to know this, but when I was with Dante, it was good for me. Not the fucking part, though that did heal a part of me, too. He's a good guy. He knew everything about you and me and never once did he expect more than no-strings. He knew it was going nowhere," I answer.

He nods and swallows hard. "Hearing that you really did fuck him—that sucks so bad."

"As opposed to seeing it?" I bite back.

He winces then nods. "You're right."

"*And* I didn't fuck fifty different people in the last few years."

"It wasn't anywhere near fifty," he replies, then realizes what he's said.

"Forty-nine?"

He scowls. "I don't know."

"Not so nice, right?"

"No, not so nice." He stands up, running his fingers through his long dark curls and then he tugs. "Fuck. How did everything get so screwed up, T?"

He paces the floor, and I sit in the rocking chair.

"Tera," he says, drawing in my attention. "I'm sorry. For all of that. For not being there. For hurting you. For not understanding what you needed when you needed it even though you told me time and time again."

"Wait. Stop." I tell him, knowing I need to address more than just Xan. "I need to say something, but I need to say it to all of you at once."

"Everyone is at the house. Let me call Jesse."

Jesse gets everyone into one room, and I let out a steadying breath.

"Guys."

"Tera!" they all greet.

"Uh, dudes. Not the time for that," Xan informs them. "She's got something to say to all of us.

"Okay," Jesse replies. "We're listening."

"This is going to be loud, and it might be ugly, but I need to get this out," I warn.

"Okay," echoes back to me through the phone.

I look at Xander from where I'm rocking, then the phone. I can't stand it. I burst from the chair. "I am so fucking mad and disappointed and resentful. You always chose the band over me. That night was *my night!* It was the equivalent of your winning the show and the contract with Nichols Records. It was *my. Night.* And you weren't there. None of you were there. Maybe if you'd been there, none of this would be happening. Maybe, if just once you felt as happy for me as I always do for you, maybe if just once you'd put me first as I always do for you, I wouldn't be so fucked up now. Maybe I wouldn't be so angry at you all."

"I need you to know. I used to blame you. All of you. I used to think it was your fault I got attacked. I resented your success with the band because I always came second to it. Always. I'm supposed to be your sister, your *wife*. How can you say you care about me when you never, not once, thought of putting me first? You all broke my heart. They may have broken my body and my spirit, but you all broke my heart."

"And then you did it again when the band, once again, pushed me back to second place. That night you celebrated that you'd hit number one. You could have done it behind closed doors, but you didn't. You didn't care enough about *my* feelings to do that for me. You have no idea what it's like to live in a fucking tin can, never being able to leave, and then never having your family around to rely on. Not once did any of you, besides Ethan, attend one of my shows. Not once. Imagine how *you'd* feel if I never went to the taping of the TV show, if I hadn't been there the night you won, if I hadn't been so understanding when you went on tour leaving me behind not once but twice my senior year of high school, and then leaving me behind to live in this box. You celebrated hitting number one, your fans celebrating with you, having the time of your life while I was here losing your baby!"

I gasp and cover my mouth.

Silence. Complete silence.

Xander's face shows shock—grief, when he whispers, "What?"

"Oh, God. I didn't mean," I sob, "I didn't mean to tell you like that."

"Holy fuck," Jesse mutters.

"You had a miscarriage?" Kennedy asks.

Tears stream down Xander's cheeks. "That night?" he whispers again.

I nod, then move to the sofa and curl up in a ball.

"Jesus," Ben says quietly.

Xander comes to me, dropping to his knees and resting his head where our baby would have been.

"No. That can't be."

"It's true," Linc tells Xan.

"Why didn't you tell me?" he asks.

I push him away. "Are you kidding? I always think of you first. Always. But you all never do! You didn't show up! And they... they beat me, they raped me, they assaulted me in ways I never imagined a person could! Where were you?"

"Then you hit number one, and it's all about you again. You partied it up—didn't once think about what 'letting your guard down' would mean to *me*. It was all about you, you, you! Every fucking one of you! You're supposed to be my family, my protectors, but this is *twice* you all chose the band over me and twice something devastating happened to me!"

The rage has set in, and it's deadly. I want to hit, tear, maim, and shred.

"How can I trust you? How can I depend on you, any of you, when I am constantly coming in second? Huh? Answer me that!"

I let out a ravaged scream just before I pick up a vase and hurl it across the room hitting the wall, the vase shattering on impact. I grab and throw, grab and throw, sobbing and screaming. I'm so angry. I reach for something else to throw, but there's nothing left on the shelf.

I stand there, breathing hard from exertion and emotion, fisted hands at my sides, the anger slowly fading. I don't see anyone or anything. I am in my own bubble, and in here I purge. I purge all of it. Anger, hate, resentment, hurt, angst, grief, disappointment…

"How could you do that to me!" I ask quietly. "How could you…?"

Now, I lose it. I sob. I sob so hard my entire body shakes.

The white-hot rage has turned to complete and utter devastation.

Chapter Fourteen

Jesse

I LOOK AT the guys then hang my head. I can't believe …

"Christ, we fucked up," I tell them soft enough that Tera can't hear.

Kennedy's silent but his eyes are wet with tears, his expression one of shame. It mirrors Ethan's.

Ben's pulling at his hair.

I swallow hard. This is on me.

"Tera?" I say softly, my voice cracking. It's all I can do not to either break down and bawl like a baby or punch a hole in the fucking wall.

She sniffles. "Yeah?" It comes out a squeak.

I close my eyes. Anguish and shame fill me.

"I am so fucking sorry. I can't even begin to tell you how sorry I am you lost the baby and that we weren't there for you. I wish you'd have told at least me when we came that day, but I understand why you didn't."

I clear my throat.

"The baby, it would've been all of ours, you know? You and Xander may have created it, but we'd have raised it as if it were our own. That's how it will always be."

"I know we were selfish and self-centered and a bunch of fucking assholes. We're all sorry for that too."

All the guys sound off their agreement.

"I want to thank you for being so honest, T. Everything you said just now, it was the truth. You emptied all your emotions, laid them bare for us to see, said everything you needed us to hear, and you were right. All of it. If we'd been there, if we'd thought of you and insisted on being there for you in LA, you wouldn't have been attacked. There are no words to tell you how sorry I am for that—how sorry we all are."

Ben clears his throat. "I've known it since it happened—that it was our fault. I can't stop seeing you lying in that hospital bed, so broken and scared. All the booze and weed in the world can't rid me of that memory and the self-contempt I feel every single day. I'm so sorry. I'm so sorry we didn't honor our promise and that you had to go through losing the baby without us. What I hate most is that you couldn't tell any of us until now. What can I do to help, Tera? What do you need? Anything, please, just don't hate me."

He said that way better than I could.

"Please don't hate any of us," I beg. "Please don't leave us again. Don't leave *me*. We need you. You're our sister, and I promise we'll never take that for granted again. Ever," I vow.

Tera sniffles again. "I'm not going to tell you it's okay. It's not. I think today will go a long way toward helping me heal so I can forgive you. You know that all of us thinking we could change anything in the past is ridiculous, right? There's no going back. Fate had it planned out for us like this. I had to go through everything for some unknown reason. Maybe one day I'll figure it out, maybe I won't, but you are my brothers, and I can't live without you either."

"Thank you, sweet Jesus," Kennedy murmurs.

"It's going to take me some time, some more therapy before there'll be any semblance of normal. I hope you understand that. It's not as easy as 'I'm sorry.'"

"Tera, we know. We understand. If you need us there for therapy, we're there. We'll do whatever it takes to be there for you. You are more important than the band," I confess. "I got caught up in the glam and glitz, fame and chicks. I hate that you went through all of this and didn't feel you could rely on us. That will *never* happen again, little sister. I promise you—and these are promises that will *not* be broken. These are blood oath promises from your big brothers."

All the guys murmur their agreement.

"We fucked up, T. I fucked up. I'm bound to do it again, but please know I am really so sorry. I would never intentionally hurt you. You *are* family to me. You know that, right?" I ask, hoarsely.

I'm met with silence.

"She's nodding," Lincoln says aloud.

I breathe out the breath I'd been holding.

Apologies come one after the other. Ben. Kennedy. Ethan.

"Thank you," she sniffles, her voice thick with tears. "I don't want to keep resenting you and sometimes hating you. That's not me, and I don't want to let that darkness win."

"We won't let it," Ben tells her.

"Enough is enough," Kennedy adds. "You want some company?"

She laughs. "I'd love some."

"We'll be there tonight—" I cut Kennedy off.

I mouth, "Tomorrow."

"Tomorrow," Xander corrects.

"Yeah, right. Tomorrow. You two have a lot to talk about," Kennedy says.

"We do. We're getting there," Tera replies.

"Good," I tell her and couldn't mean anything more. "See you tomorrow afternoon, Mackenzies—and Linc."

"See you then," Tera replies.

When the call ends I run to the bathroom and vomit. When I can't throw up anymore, I stand on shaky legs in front of the mirror above the sink. I can't look at myself. I can't.

I rinse my mouth, then brush my teeth.

I still can't look.

I splash my face with cold water.

When I still can't look, I let the first tear of shame fall. Then come tears of regret.

Ethan knocks, and I turn to him.

"You okay, man?"

"No. So many wrong decisions, E. And they're all on me."

"Nah. If we didn't agree we would've spoken up. No one did."

I nod, watching the water run, swirl down the drain. I splash my face once more then turn the water off.

I force myself to look in the mirror. Who I see isn't the same guy who looked in the mirror this morning. I'm different, forever changed because of the consequences of my actions.

I slide my gaze to Ethan.

"This isn't going to happen again. To anyone. Ever. It's time we grow the fuck up and act responsibly. It isn't just us—it never was, and I hate that we lost sight of that," I confess.

"It's not gonna happen again," Ben tells me from where he stands behind Ethan.

"We learned a bitter lesson today. We almost lost our baby sister—as it is we lost our niece or nephew and Tera's been suffering in silence because she couldn't depend on us to be there for her," Kennedy reiterates. "That won't happen again on my watch."

"Mine either," Ethan agrees.

"Eyes wide open, boys," I tell them. I turn to face them. "Today we awoke from a dream life—one free of consequence. Today we took off the blinders. Today we see what we did. Today we see and know what we need to do next."

"Today we become men."

Chapter Fifteen

Xander

THE PHONE CALL ends, Linc leaves the room, and it's just Tera and me. I hold her on my lap, rocking in the chair, too afraid to let go.

All the things she said... I am such a bastard. I really don't deserve her.

I can't believe I fell for that "settled" bullshit. I should have known better. I should have known Tera better than that. I should have known *us* better than that.

"Tera... I know it's been said a million times today, but I am *so god damn sorry*. If you hadn't felt obligated to talk to me on the phone that night, you wouldn't have stayed behind, and you'd have been okay. But I was so fucking needy, missing you like crazy, wanting to hear everything I hadn't been there to experience with you. I should have just gone. I was on that stage in some dive venue, hammering away on the drums on instinct rather than the passion I usually play with, and it was all because I knew I should have been *there*. We all knew. We nearly took off before the show. When I got that call from the hospital…" my voice cracks and I bury my face in her neck as the tears fall.

"They didn't know if you'd make it. I thought I'd lost you and it would've been all my fucking fault. We couldn't get there fast enough. It seemed like forever, and when we got there, you were in surgery. The nurses could only tell us it was touch and go."

"Then Winters showed up with his dad. He was so pale, somber. He couldn't even talk. He just kept nodding or staring into space. When his dad told me you'd done a random dial and it was Carter, I understood why he was a zombie. How he held it together, T. I don't know. He is strong as all hell. I didn't know whether I should cry, find someone to beat the hell out of, or what… so I went and sat in the chapel until Dad got there," I confess. Tera looks at me in surprise.

"I know we've never been real religious, but in that moment I knew I needed help from a higher power and The Big Man was the only one listening, it seemed. I prayed. I prayed my ass off. I made deals that were insane, and I'm sure He gets that a lot, but I meant them. I'd have done anything, *anything* in that moment to trade places with you so you never knew a moment's pain or fear."

"But if wishes were dollars I'd be a millionaire… isn't that how it goes?" I'm rambling. She doesn't care. She's just listening, and she's calming down.

"When I saw…" my voice cracks again, so I clear my throat. "When I saw you in that bed, hooked up to all of those machines, so battered and bruised, and knowing you were assaulted," I sob, "I will never forgive myself for that. Never. Rationally I know it's no one's fault, it just happened, it was random, but I can't shake the feeling that the blame falls on my shoulders."

"Xan, I think you need some counseling, too. Earlier when I was pissed, I would have reveled in your guilt, but you shouldn't have lived with this for over *five years*. Xander, say you'll talk to someone. Please," she asks.

In this moment I'd give her the world if I could.

I nod. "I will. The guys need it too. We all know the guilt is there. It's eating us alive. It's why Ben drinks like he does. It's why Jesse fucks every chick he can. It's why Kennedy never sets down his guitar—not even when he sleeps. It's why Ethan has been screwing and clinging to random chicks. It's why I keep self-destructing. We know. We welcomed it… until now."

"I think, maybe, that's why you kept me at arm's length. Don't—" she says when I go to deny it. "It's not just you. It's all of you. I knew there was a reason. I just didn't know why."

I nod. "We need a really good fucking shrink, Tera."

She snickers. "Yeah, we do. Every single one of us."

"Why can't we all be like Linc and just get our aggression, guilt, and everything else out when we kick the shit out of someone in the ring?" I ask.

"Because you're all a bunch of pussies and would get your asses handed to you," Linc tells me from where he stands in the kitchen.

I didn't even see him walk in there.

"Likely, but the physical pain would be a welcomed respite from the emotional shit. This is some brutal hell we're living in," I confess.

"Welcome to my world," Tera tells me.

"I know," I tell her, looking into her beautiful brown eyes. "I would do anything to carry your burden, T. Anything. I can't stand that all of this happened to you. It hurts so much I ache with it. It frustrates the hell out of me."

She nods.

"Please, Tera, forgive me. Please. Maybe not today, but try? I don't ever want to be without you again. You are my world, and when you're not in it, I don't want to be there," I confess.

"Oh, Xan." She hugs me, and I hug her back, tight, holding on for dear life. "I'm working on it. I think this was a positive step, and one I've obviously needed for a long time."

Linc sweeps up more glass into the dustpan. "You think?"

She doesn't even look embarrassed nor should she.

"I think that was therapeutic for you, babe. Was it my face you were aiming at?" I ask.

Linc snorts. "More like your dick, you fucker."

Tera snorts in return. "I didn't see anything. Just red, then it turned white. It was like white-hot rage. It's not something I feel often."

"Thank fuck," Linc mutters, continuing to clean up the glass.

"I'm sorry, Linc," Tera says.

Linc shakes his head. "Don't you dare apologize to me, baby sister. You needed this so fucking bad. I could see it all eating away at you. Yeah, you talked it over with your head shrinker, but you never told the right people. Finally. Finally, I think you'll be able to heal."

Tera nods.

"And you," Linc says pointing at me.

Oh, fucking hell.

"You fuck up with my sister again, and I'll break more than your nose, pretty boy. I'll fuck you up so bad you'll pray for death, but I'll never give you that out. *She* didn't get it, so neither do *you*. She's stronger than all five of you *Falling Down* pussies put together. If any of that shit happened to you, you'd be whining every minute of every day for the rest of your life. But not Tera. Hell fucking no, not Tera. She's still got shit to work on, but she's kicking ass and taking names. Workin' it out like a boss, baby sister," Linc says, then goes back to sweeping up the glass.

That's a lot of glass. She threw a lot of shit.

"I'm so proud of you, Tera. For today. For yesterday. For every day before and the ones still to come. I admire your strength and will to go on. Anyone else would've given up," I state.

"Maybe," she replies. "But I'm not anyone else."

"No, you sure aren't. You're the one and only Tera Louise Ramirez Mackenzie."

"I'm exhausted."

I sigh with her as she rests her head against my shoulder. "Me too."

"I'm making you some of that mandarin tea shit," Linc shouts.

"He takes care of me when I lose my shit. Without him, I'd have had to take it all out on Shea, and she'd have found you and castrated you before she murdered you," she states matter-of-factly.

"Yikes. I admit I'm more than a little afraid of Shea. She's truly wicked."

Tera yawns. "I want you to know, Xan, I never slept with Carter... wait. I did *sleep* with him. I never had sex with him. We came up here and talked, fell asleep, and woke up to Lincoln's bellowing."

Thank you, Jesus. I knew you were listening! "I thought for sure you did and that you'd go back to him."

"Looks like I was the only one who learned the first time around. It wasn't him I wanted, remember? It was you. It is you."

"Even after... everything. All my fuckups... the sex tape?"

"That sex tape still grates something fierce, but yeah, Xan. Even after."

"Can I kiss you now?"

"You better."

We kiss the day away. We talk—really talk like we used to. She tells everything, and I do the same. I tell her honestly about Jesse and the threesomes we've done together. She confesses that while the thought of a threesome is hot, she could never do it. She could never screw Jesse, and she could never be with another guy in front of me.

It'd kill me, and she knows it. I can't imagine what it feels like for her to have seen me with all those models, to have watched the tape. God. I'd kill a fucker.

I carry her to her room where we lay facing each other, legs intertwined, holding hands—not wanting to let go. I don't make any moves on her. We're too fragile for that. We just keep kissing and holding one another until we fall asleep

This is where I belong. Here, with my wife. I will never go another day without her in my life. Never.

Chapter Sixteen

Tera

WE SETTLE INTO a comfortable life. Xander visits me as often as he can, sometimes staying weeks at a time. Jesse, Ben, Kennedy, and Ethan show up out of the blue when Xander stays for lengthier periods of time. It's like they can't be apart that long.

They go through therapy sessions with me—sometimes here and sometimes via Skype. It's helping all of us so much. I can see they're lighter than when they came here the first time after I "purged", and it makes me so happy.

What's even better is, I'm learning to be happy again.

When they come to one of my shows, no one there recognizes them, and I laugh when they're almost insulted by it.

"Fuck these people," Jesse curses, all affronted. "How do they not know who we are? We're *Falling Down*, motherfuckers!"

I laugh at his outrage. "These are artistic people. They likely don't do 'rockstar.'"

"Losers, every one of them," Jesse insists. Then he goes on to tell me how they're artists, and in the end, I let him win. He's got a point… just not the same kind I was trying to make.

But that's okay. We've learned to compromise. We've learned to negotiate when we need to. We've learned to be family again.

One night after we make love, I ask Xander if he's upset with me for not being able to be with him outside of my comfort zone.

"Never. I've lived without you once, Tera. I'll take you any way I can get you for as long as you'll let me," he assures me.

It's then that I finally start to live—*really* live again. It's then that I begin to believe in happily ever after again. It's then I allow myself to be completely happy and whole with my family and the man I love.

THE PRESENT

Chapter Seventeen

Tera

"How is Jamie able to afford a jet?" I ask Linc. Jamie "Jabs" Royal is one of Linc's fighter buddies. Their underground isn't so "underground" anymore. They've become very popular, but they like this mid-level status they're at.

I, personally, think Linc could kick some serious ass at the UFC level, but he keeps telling me he's not in it for the fame. Every time he says it, I roll my eyes. He *loves* the attention, but then again he does like his privacy.

"He's made investments," Linc answers as the car we hired drives us to the airport.

"You've made investments," I remind him.

"I have," he agrees.

"And?" I prod.

He smirks. "I could buy a jet if I wanted to. But I don't travel enough to justify the expense. Royal is always going somewhere."

I nod. "With his harem of sluts."

Linc laughs. "They're not sluts, T. They're his girlfriends."

I roll my eyes—again. "Girlfriends," I say making quotes with my fingers. "He should be saying, girl*friend*. Not plural."

"He is who he is," Linc tells me with a shrug.

"Yeah, well."

We fall into a comfortable silence, and I take in the sights—sights I haven't been able to enjoy for over a decade. Sights I took for granted and never will again.

"Look at that skyline. It's so beautiful," I tell Linc, pointing out the sunrise.

He grunts and takes another drink of his coffee.

"You should learn to appreciate it. You could be like me and not get to see it in forever," I remind him.

"I appreciate it. I'm just not looking forward to flying."

Linc's never liked flying—not even when we were kids. "I told you, we could have taken the train or gone on a road trip."

"Hell no. There is no way you'd be able to handle being on a cramped train for that long no matter how much therapy you've had. *I* have issues with it. And road trip? With you? Listening to your music? Fuck the fuck no. You'd turn on some Bieber or some shit like that," he replies.

"Maybe I'd play some Biebs, but at least I wouldn't play she who shall not be named," I tease.

"All you gotta say is 'Evil' and I know who you mean. Ben knew what he was doing when he nicknamed her that."

I nod. "True story."

"Are you anxious, Tera?" Linc asks.

I shrug a shoulder. "Of course, I am. I wouldn't be me if I weren't, but I'll be okay. I have my anxiety exercises, and it's really just the airport that I'll have issues with."

"Both here and there."

"Here more than there. I'll be too excited when we get there to think much about where we are and who's around," I fib.

"Lies. You'll think. You'll worry. You'll fret. But you'll make it through because you're the strongest you've been since the attack."

"It's not easy. It won't get easier. I'll always have the anxiety, and that really sucks. I hate that people did this to me. I hate that people are still doing this to others. I hate that it's more commonplace than it was when it happened to me and that people have actually gotten so used to it happening they aren't even as outraged anymore."

"I hear ya, baby sister. The world has become a fucked up place. All we can do is try to make it better instead of worse."

"We're here already?" I ask, yawning. That decaf coffee didn't help. Ugh, decaf.

We get our luggage, and Linc takes care of everything. I take a seat in one of the chairs in the terminal and begin the wait to board the plane headed to Los Angeles—and Xander.

I people watch. It's interesting watching people, trying to figure out where they're from or where they're going. It was part of my therapy when I got to the point I could do it, to look at people—I mean *really* look at people and imagine what they're thinking or doing, where they're going, etc.

A businessman in a well-tailored navy suit hurries down the walkway, weaving effortlessly between the other travelers. He's an experienced traveler, I deduce. He's probably hopping a plane to DC for some political thing. He carries himself like a politician or lawyer.

"What're you doing?" Linc asks.

"People watching."

"No one's going to hurt you, T."

I thought that once, too. I give him a forced smile. "Not with you here, my hulk-like brother."

He flexes his arm then smacks the muscle with his other hand. "No way they'd get through me."

I snort when I notice more than one woman standing and staring.

"Stop flexing. Either that or start handing out drool rags," I tease.

Linc looks up and chuckles. He nods at the women. "Ladies."

"I'm surprised they didn't giggle like schoolgirls."

Linc wiggles his eyebrows. "Wouldn't be the first time."

"Ack," I reply. Yeah, my brother has muscles upon muscles, and I can see the appeal. I suppose he's not bad looking in a bad boy kind of way.

"Stop staring," Linc tells me.

I shrug. "Just trying to see what they see."

He leans back in his chair. "I'm pure awesome from head to toe."

I laugh. "You stole that from Xander, didn't you?"

He shakes his head. "Nope, just expanded it and added 'from head to toe.'"

"Well done, big brother. Well done."

Someone sits in the bank of chairs behind mine I smell it—whiskey on their breath and cigarette smoke that clings to their clothes and hair. It reminds me of *them*. I get icy, numb from fear. I sit and listen. Will he say something?

"Stop, Tera. It's not him," he says.

And it's not—*him*. *Them*.

I snap my anxiety wristband, reminding myself I am in control, not my anxiety. I snap it again and reassure myself no one's going to hurt me. I snap it a third and final time, then close my eyes and take calming breaths just as I learned in therapy. In through the nose, out through the mouth. Again. Again. Again. I finally feel calm.

"Royal's got someone coming with one of those cart things. He refuses to let, and I quote, 'your hot sister walk so far. That wouldn't be gentlemanly.'" Linc scoffs. "That guy has had the hots for you since the day I met him."

I laugh. "He is hot and muscular and sweet—"

Linc heckles when I say the word sweet.

"But I'm not in the market for a new man. I've already got one," I answer.

Linc pauses and looks down at me. "Do you?"

"Good question, big brother."

"This might be more difficult than you think."

"Yeah, I know. He's got an amazing life going on. He's in love with Jesse's wife. He plays daddy to their babies. He may not have room or want to make room for me anymore." I sigh, then straighten my shoulders. "Know what? He doesn't get a choice. He asked me to go there and I worked my ass off to be able to get there, so now he's gonna get what he asked for."

Linc whistles. "Tough words."

"It's Xan, Linc. What we have? That doesn't disappear no matter how long we've to live on different coasts. Besides, he just came to visit."

"I hope you're right. Ah, here's our ride. Let's go get your husband."

I think I've got a right to be a little afraid and less than confident right now. After all, I was the one who chose to live my life there. But, I did go through hell to get where I am now. Everything I do, everything I've done, it's all for us.

Chapter Eighteen

Tera

SHIT. I'M NERVOUS. Linc and I are walking up to the door of this huge mansion Xan calls Casa Falling Down and I can't help it. My jaw drops. I don't belong here. This… this is *so much*. I'm the girl from the wrong side of the tracks and Xan's always been from the rich side. Right now, I'm feeling that distance, even if I've made more than a good living for myself.

"Relax, Tera," Linc says.

I wipe my hands on my jeans. "Easy for you to say. This is it. Do or die. Yes or no. Either he's gonna be happy to see me or he's gonna throw me out."

"Jesus. Stop freaking out. He *asked* you to come here, remember?"

"Yeah, sure, *two years ago!*" I retort.

"Do you really think he'd take it back?" Linc asks.

I shrug. I've heard about his family. I've heard about Lucy. I know all about her and I don't like it. But then, there are things he doesn't like about my life, either—though, those things, or people, as they were, have been left behind.

Linc presses the doorbell. We hear voices—lots and lots of voices. Loud voices. I step a little to the left, slightly behind Linc.

"It'll be all right," he encourages.

I look up to meet his eyes. "What if it's not?"

"Then, little sister, we leave," he says quietly.

"I can't ask you to do that again."

"You aren't, and you never did. That was my decision, and this would be as well," he corrects.

"But what about you and –"

I'm cut off when the door opens and a cute little pixie of a girl greets us.

"Merry Christmas!" she shouts.

"Merry Christmas," Linc and I answer with grins.

"Oh boy," I whisper as Jace Warner opens the door further.

"Didn't we just talk about opening the door by yourself, Kadi?"

"Daddy," she says, clearly exasperated. "Uncle Jesse said we have more security than Fort Knox. I think I'm safe."

Jace laughs as he looks up at us. "Seven going on thirty."

Linc and I laugh.

"Can I help you?" Jace asks, scratching the back of his head.

"Um…" I begin, a little star struck. "We're looking for Xander and the guys."

"We're friends, not stalkers," Linc clarifies.

Jace nods. "Yeah, there's no way you'd make it past security if you weren't on the list."

Linc nudges me with his elbow. "See? We're on the list."

I nod stiffly. I'm not feeling real reassured right now.

Jace opens the door even further. "Come in, come in. Join the chaos that is CFD on Christmas morning." Then he extends his hand. "Jace Warner."

"Uh, yeah, I know who you are." I'm freaking star-struck. My mouth is hanging open and there's nothing I can do to stop it.

Linc nudges me again and Jace smirks. Linc holds out his hand. "Linc Ramirez."

Jace's eyes widen. "No shit? Dude, welcome home."

"I take it the guys talk about us?" Linc probes.

"Oh yeah. For sure. And you are?" he asks me.

"Oh. Duh. I'm Tera Mackenzie."

"Happy to meet you—wait. Wait, wait, wait." He holds up his hands and cocks his head to the side, eyes wide. "Did you just say *Mackenzie?!*"

I huff. "I'm guessing he didn't tell you that part, huh?"

Jace scratches the back of his head again. "No, can't say he has."

"Isn't that just like a man," I bite out, stepping into the house.

"So… you're Xander's *wife?*" Jace asks.

When I answer with a simple, "Yes," the entire household goes quiet.

"Tera?!" I hear someone yell. "Where is that girl?" Jesse.

He comes striding out of a room with Christmas bows stuck all over his head and… a bathrobe? He is totally domesticated. Whoa.

"There she is," he shouts. When he spots Linc, his grin gets even wider, those dimples winking. Oh, Jesse Kingston is still as pretty as ever.

He lifts me up and twirls me in a hug. "It's damn good to see you."

"You, too," I tell him, tears filling my eyes. "I've missed you," I whisper.

"I've missed you, too, little one. I'm so glad you're here. He is going to go nuts," Jesse informs me as he sets me down.

"Yeah?" I ask, hopeful.

Jesse nods. "He's been waiting."

I nod. "I had things to work out first."

"You don't ever have to explain yourself to me. And you, you son of a bitch," he says to Linc, grabbing him into one of those man hugs where they slap each other's backs.

"Jesse. You fucker," Linc replies.

"Ah, I feel the love," Kennedy says as he walks up and hugs me tight, so tight. I hug him just as close. I breathe him in.

"You still smell like home, Kennedy," I tell him.

"I *am* your home. Never forget it. Xan is gonna lose his shit," Kennedy tells me with one of his rare huge smiles.

"Fucker," Linc greets Kennedy.

Ethan walks up and doesn't say a word. He just wraps his arms around me, burying his face into my neck. I rest my cheek on his head.

"Oh, Ethan," I say, not even bothering to hold back the tears now. It's a losing battle.

"Tera," he whispers. "Thank you."

"I'm sorry it took so long," I reply.

"You're here now. That's all that matters," Ethan tells me, standing up, wiping his eyes. He looks to Linc and smirks. "Linc."

Linc pulls him into a hug, but this one doesn't have any of the slapping he had with Jesse and Kennedy. This one is an eye-closing, heart-thumping hug. I sigh inwardly. I knew it.

"Ethan," Linc murmurs.

They step back and just look at one another. No one's saying much of anything, yet the room is full of so many people. I look to the left and there's my mom.

"Mama!" I shout, running to her.

"Mija," she replies through tears. Then she continues on in

Spanish, telling me how much she's missed me. How beautiful I am. How much Xander needs me so he'll smile again.

The scent of fresh earth and flowers wafts over me and my smile widens, my heart happy. I feel *home.* Content.

"Papa," I whisper, turning to hug him tight. He looks the same, just a little grayer hair around the edges. But this is my papa.

"Baby girl. It's about time," he tells me.

We step back and that's when I realize the room is full of people, but no Xander.

I turn to Mama and Papa. "I'm on a mission."

"Go, go," Mama urges with a smile and a tear in her eye. "It is time."

"All right, boys," I say to Kennedy and Ethan. "Lead me to my husband."

I hear feminine gasps, and I cringe inwardly. That is not going to go over well. Xander is in so much trouble, and we're going to have so much to explain.

But first, Xander.

"This way," Kennedy says, taking my hand and leading me up the stairs, Ethan trailing behind with Linc.

I look at the painting at the top of the stairs.

"That's one of mine! When did you get this? This was from my first show."

Kennedy shrugs. "You gotta ask Jesse."

"Jesse," I whisper and smile. *They have some of my work hanging in their home. A piece of me was here all along.*

Ethan chuckles. "This… we gotta get this on camera."

"All set," Kennedy tells him, holding his phone. "I started rolling when Mrs. M spotted Tera."

"Thank you," I tell him.

"Of course. Now, let's do it this way. You stay right here. His room is on the other side of this wall, the door just around the corner. Let me and Ethan fuck with him a bit, first?" Kennedy asks.

"Far be it from me to deny you your mischief," I tell him with a snicker. I wipe my sweaty palms on my jeans again. I'm so nervous. I've never been here. Yes, I've gone to him before at hotels or places he asked me to go before the attack, but never here to his home. The agoraphobia prevented that from happening, and truth be told, I'd been waiting for him to ask me to be with him. I told Dr. Wilson, my therapist, about the waiting and when she asked me why. I told her the truth: I wasn't sure he wanted me the way he once did. I wasn't sure he'd want me here now that he has a new family. I wasn't and still am unsure if I'll fit in.

Those are things I'm here to find out, as well.

"Dude, you up?" Ethan bellows and pounds on the door. I have to stifle my laugh. I hear stomping, and Ethan winks at me.

Linc chuckles silently, looking like the little boy he once was when he was up to no good.

"Fuck, man. If I weren't, I'd be pissed," Xander growls, opening the door. I can smell his body wash from here and my heart flutters, my stomach flips and flops, my breath catches in my throat.

I'm here. In his house. What's he going to think? What will he feel? Happiness? Annoyance?

"There's a chick here to see you," Ethan announces.

"Fuck that. It's family time and the fucking holiday. Send whoever it is away," Xander bites out.

Well. That stings some now, doesn't it? I wonder, if it wasn't family time and a holiday, would he still be fucking other women? Has he been?

Kennedy smirks. "You sure you wanna do that? She's super fucking hot, man."

Xander sighs. "Hot chicks are a dime a dozen. I'm not in the mood for a random, okay? I've got my day planned out, and it doesn't include dealing with a stranger."

Ethan gives Xan a look, like he's trying to telepathically tell him it's me. "You *know* her."

Linc snickers.

I hear a rustling of clothing.

Ethan blinks. "You know her *well.*"

I bite my lip to stop from laughing out loud. This is hilarious.

"Not interested."

Yes! I fist pump the air and Kennedy snickers.

"Dude, you might want to—" Ethan begins.

"No. The answer is no. I don't want to talk to some chick. No," Xander says emphatically.

Ethan winks and tilts his head. Oh boy. That's my cue.

"Not even if that *chick* is your *wife?*" I ask as I walk up and lean against the doorjamb.

I hear him, my Xan, my husband, my heart, audibly gasp and it both swells and breaks my heart. It hurts to know how I've disappointed him.

"*Tera,*" Xander whispers.

Chapter Nineteen

Lucy

I KNEW THIS day would come, when we'd meet her, but I'm not ready. I'm angry and hurt and my heart hurts. I had no warning.

When they finish walking up the stairs, I look to Sera. "Watch the kids?"

It sounds like a question, but it's really not. I don't even wait for an answer before grabbing Jesse's hand and pulling him to our suite.

Have you ever been so frustrated you wanted to cry? That's me right now. But I need to get my angry out first.

Jesse shuts the door and leans back against the wall—waiting.

"I knew. I knew about her. He mentioned her name. I knew

she meant everything to him." I let out a huff of exasperation and begin pacing. "Why didn't either of you tell me!"

Jesse doesn't flinch, but I see remorse in his eyes.

"It wasn't my story to tell, Cupcake."

"I'm your *wife!* We have no secrets from one another—or, at least, that's what I thought." The tears are threatening now, but I push them back.

"Tera and Xander made a deal when we went on the road," Jesse explains.

"What kind of deal?"

He sighs. "All I know is they were keeping their relationship private, so Tera wouldn't be bombarded by fans or the press. Then something happened—something horrible, and that made the deal solid—for all of us. We all made promises. No one said anything about them being married. No one."

"You could have told me!" I yell. A tear slips free. "*He* should have told me."

"Try to understand, Luce. When that something bad happened, he didn't know if they'd ever live the life of a traditional husband and wife. Honestly, I'm amazed she's here. Not because she doesn't love him—she does. She fucking loves that guy like crazy. But because of what happened," Jesse tells me, wiping away my tears.

"You can't tell me that either, huh?"

"No. That's not—"

"Your story to tell. I know." I know it's not fair to take my anger and frustration out on him. I know, but still I snap at him.

"Luce…"

"She just showed up. No one knew. No one was prepared—*I* wasn't prepared, and I really, really needed to prepare for that, for this. This… it hurts, Jesse," I admit.

He tries to pull me into a hug, but I pull back, my angry not gone yet.

"He's ours! Damn it, Jesse, he's *ours*! He should have told me. How could he not tell me something like this? And then she shows up. Did he know?" I look up at the ceiling and raise my fisted hands to my chest, my gaze lowers to meet Jesse's. "He's *ours!*"

Jesse walks up slowly, holding my face in his hands, his thumbs wiping my tears.

"You have to understand, Cupcake. He was hers, first."

And that's all it takes. I burst into tears. It's not rational, my thinking Xander is ours, but that's how I feel.

"Do you think he'd be happy like this forever, Luce? Having no one of his own? Because, in reality, you're mine and I'm yours. He's part of us—yes, but he's not *part* of us. He deserves his own happiness and love, doesn't he?" he asks.

I nod. "Yes. But it hurts."

Jesse sighs. "I know, Luce. I know. I know you love him. Maybe not how you love me, but you love him. I know he loves you, too. I know it, and I know you can't help how you feel. I know you'd never act on it—either of you, but it still sucks for me."

"I'm sorry," I whisper.

"Don't be sorry, Luce. I get it. Xan's one of those guys who everyone loves. If I swung that way, I'd probably fall in love with him, too."

"You've already got the bromance going on," I remind him.

"Yeah, there's that." He sighs again while he rubs my back and holds me to him. "I'm sure he didn't know she was coming. He'd have mentioned it. He'd have talked it out before she got here. You know Xan would never hurt you."

"I know."

"But she's here, Luce, and she's his wife. They've been apart since we started touring. Sure, he'd go stay with her for weekends, weeks, or months, but their relationship wasn't a real marriage for a long time. She's here now to see if that's possible. It's going to be hard, and it's going to hurt your feelings, but he deserves happiness, and so does she."

"I know. I do. And I want him to be happy, but this is going to be a lot to get used to," I tell him honestly, looking up into those whiskey-colored eyes that see to my soul.

"I get it, Luce, and I'm here for you to lean on."

"I love you, Jesse. I love you like no one else," I remind him.

"I know, Cupcake. I love you, too."

Chapter Twenty

Tera

I GRIN.

He reaches out, touching my face, my shoulders, my hips, my ass, and my boobs. I snicker.

"She's real," he says, looking over my shoulder at Kennedy.

I grab his t-shirt in my fist and pull him to me. I nod. "I'm here. Now, what are you gonna do about it?" Oh, those are mighty big words for someone shaking so hard inside I'm afraid I might shatter.

He pulls me in and kisses me softly, so softly I can barely feel it. He breathes out my name like a prayer and a tear slips from my eye.

Then he *really* kisses me. All lips and tongues and hands. We're so rushed and harried, our teeth hit. We both lean back and laugh.

"I haven't had that happen since the first time I kissed you," Xan tells me.

"I love that it happened with me both times," I tell him honestly.

"Dude," my brother bellows, shoving me to the side, wrapping his arms around Xander, lifting him and bouncing him up and down. "How's my bro-in-law?"

Xan tries to catch his breath when Linc sets him down.

"I'm good, now that you're letting me breathe again."

Linc grins. "I missed you, ya fucker."

Xan laughs. "Oh, you're gonna be in so much trouble in this house, Linc."

"What do you mean?" Linc asks.

Kennedy and Ethan chuckle.

"We've got a swear jar. Fuck costs a buck. All the others, fifty cents," Ethan tells him.

"You're fucking kidding me," Linc replies.

Ethan laughs. "Nope. Serious as a heart attack, man. And Kadi? The little girl who answered the door?"

Linc nods.

"She's strict, man. She won't let it slide, *at all*. I'm her favorite, and she makes me pay every time," Ethan tells him.

"Well, shit. I need to get some singles and quarters. Reminds me of when we used to go to the arcade. Remember that shit?" Linc asks.

"I think Linc's going to pay the kids' college tuition all by himself," Kennedy teases.

Linc rubs his hand over his short black hair. "Good thing I've got money, or I'd have to take out a loan."

"You've got money?" Kennedy asks.

Of all the guys, Kennedy came around the least. I think it was too hard for him each time we said goodbye. Ethan kept in touch the most and stopped by for a weekend or a week. Jesse and Ben popped in now and again before they got married and Jesse's wife had the babies.

"He's been doing a higher level of the underground fighting than he'd been doing before," Ethan informs Kennedy.

"No shit?"

Linc nods.

Kennedy whistles. "That explains you being built like a fucking tank. Tell me about this fighting."

"Dude," Linc begins as they turn to walk away, "It's awesome."

Xander and I just stare at one another, grinning like dorks.

"You came," he says, breaking the silence.

I nod. "I said 'yes.'"

He nods in return. "You did. Did you do okay getting here?"

"Yep. We used one of Linc's friend's planes. I just couldn't do commercial. Not yet," I tell him honestly.

"Baby, you've come such a long way in such a short time. I'm so fucking proud of you," he tells me, smiling wide, his dimples making an appearance.

My heart sighs. Oh, how I've missed him.

"Thanks."

"Now, get in here," he says quickly, grabbing my arm and pulling me into his room. He shuts the door and locks it.

I turn around, slowly backing away as he advances toward me like a predator.

"It's been a long damn time, Tera. There's going to be nothing romantic or smooth about this first time. I'm gonna fuck you hard and fast until you scream my name," he tells me, his eyes filled with purpose and desire.

"Is that all?" I taunt.

"Hell no! Then I'm gonna fuck you again. Maybe a couple more times before I can go slow and gentle enough to make love to you. I've got a big need for you, wife. Think you can handle it?"

I roll my eyes. "Please."

"You don't need to beg, baby. Not yet. That'll come later," Xan says with a smirk.

"You're awfully sure of yourself."

He wraps me up in his arms and stares into my eyes. "You're here. You're finally here. I knew the day you came to me you'd be here to stay. Welcome home, wife."

It's then that I hug him tight and begin to cry.

Chapter Twenty-One

Xander

I DON'T KNOW what I did, but Tera's crying her heart out against my chest.

"What's wrong, babe?" I ask. She says something through her sobs that is absolutely incoherent. "Babe. Shh. Just take deep, steady breaths." I'm trying to soothe her with my words while my hands rub circles on her back.

"Whatever it is, we'll work it out," I tell her.

"I'm afraid," she sobs.

"Of what?"

She sniffles. "That I took too long. That I won't fit in. That they won't accept me. That we won't be compatible anymore."

"Oh, is that all?" I tease.

She pushes my shoulder then wipes her tears. "It's not funny, Xan. What if…"

I press my index finger against her lips. "You could 'what if' all day long and worry yourself into a frenzy, but at the end of the day the only way to find out 'what if' is to do it. That's what we're doing. Right here. Right now."

She sniffles again. "Maybe, but—"

I shush her again. "No maybe. No but. Just right now, just this minute. Not tomorrow or the next day."

She huffs. "When did you become a grown up?"

I laugh. "Right around the time I lost you."

Her face scrunches up. "You're going to make me cry again."

I chuckle. "No more crying. Unless it's happy tears. Then you can cry."

I rest my hands on her cheeks and tip her head back so she's looking at me.

"We will get through this and come out even better than we are right now. I promise you."

"Don't make promises you can't keep, Xan," she whispers.

"I never do." I take a deep breath. I don't want her to worry. She just got here. I don't want her to be afraid—of me, of us. "Tera."

She blinks.

"Do you love me?" I ask, a little afraid of the answer because, if she doesn't, she's going to make a liar out of me. If she doesn't love me, there's no way I can keep that promise to her.

"Of course, I love you, Xan. You're everything."

Relief pours through me, but I do my best to mask it. Does it make me a hypocrite that I'm a little afraid but I don't want her to be? Yep. Sure does. But she has nothing to fear from me. I'm still all in. I always have been.

"A better question is: Are you *in* love with me? Do you love me like you used to?" I ask, showing her my cards. I'll share every single piece of me with her if her answer is yes.

She shakes her head. "No, I don't."

My heart sinks. Well… fuck.

One of her hands rests against my cheek, her eyes go soft, and my stomach flips over. Always with her.

"I love you more, Xan."

I don't even hide the shaky breath that I release. I rest my forehead against hers. "You had me worried for a minute."

"Oh—"

"Shh," I silence her with my index finger against her lips. "I *know* now." I kiss her lips softly. "I'm not the same guy I used to be, Tera. A lot of things about me have changed, things you couldn't have seen when I came to visit."

She nods. "I know. That's part of what I'm afraid of."

"But… why? My love for you hasn't changed."

"Maybe not, but like you said, you've changed—and I haven't. Maybe we're too different now."

"Tera. Stop. Relax. It's me. It's *us*. We've never had problems being together and we won't now, either."

She eyes me warily. "How can you—"

I place my index finger over her lips—again.

"I just do. Stop thinking, okay? Just… for once in a long fucking time, just *be*. Be with me," I plead.

She smirks. "That's why I'm here."

"I'm so fucking glad you're here, baby."

"Me too," she breathes against my lips then kisses me softly. "But, uh, speaking of my being here," she begins, wincing a bit, "you didn't tell everyone we're married and the women downstairs who, from the photos you've shared with me, are Lucy, Summer, and Nicole, well, they were throwing daggers at their men with their eyes. I *think* maybe you should try to smooth things over before we get naked."

"Hell no. They can handle their own women. We'll talk to them when we come up for air. Until then, we're staying in here. Just you and me. I've waited so long for this day, I won't let anything ruin it."

I breathe her in.

"You're here. You're really here."

Finally.

Write SEX

Chapter Twenty-Two

Xander

WE TAKE A quick shower, Tera pinning up her long locks so as to not get them wet. I tried to bang her again in the shower, but she wasn't having any of it.

Something's different about her. It's not just that she's happier...

I watch her, look at my wife, *really* look at her. She's curvier. Sexier. Prettier.

She's trying to hook her bra and getting frustrated when it doesn't latch right away.

"Here, let me," I offer. When it's closed, I reach around and cup her breasts. She's always had an incredible rack, but... wait.

"I'm not feeling so well," she tells me, her face pale, beads of sweat on her brow.

"Do you want some ginger ale or something? Mrs. M swears by that," I offer.

She shakes her head, her eyes widen, and she books it to the bathroom. She barely makes it to the toilet before she starts throwing up. I'm not gonna lie. Before the K-Quads, I probably would've puked right along with her. But having four puking and shitting machines around, well, it toughens a person up.

But seeing her retch like this, dry heaving.

I wet a cloth and wipe her forehead.

"Are you okay? Do you need to rest? Was it from flying, do you think?" I keep firing off questions. It can't be food. She's got nothing in her stomach. Maybe that's the problem.

She shakes her head and gasps for breath.

"Maybe you need to eat something."

When she's done, tears run down her cheeks, her face is now red, and she looks exhausted.

"Come here, woman. Let's rinse your mouth."

I hand her a cup of water, a toothbrush, toothpaste, and mouthwash.

"There's some medication in the cabinet from when I had food poisoning. Do you want some of that? There's some of that pink chalky shit in there, too," I offer.

"No, no. This is good. I just need to get this taste out of my mouth."

I nod.

"Then I want to talk to you about something."

"If it's about the family, it'll be okay. They're upset now, yeah, but once we explain everything it'll be okay. And we don't have to go into too much detail if you're not comfortable with that. I mean, they're strangers to you at this point—"

"Not really," she says, cutting me off. "You've told me so much over the years, I feel as if I know them already. But, I am a stranger to them. I'll be okay with details. Will they, do you think?" she asks.

I shrug. "I don't see why not. I guess we'll just warn them, you know?"

She nods. "Especially Lucy, seeing as she's gone through something like that, too."

"Yeah, she has. She's kept a lot of that between her and Jesse. I only know parts. I respected that because I know from everything you've been through that talking about it to other people can't be easy."

"It's not. It's really not." She rinses her mouth.

We finish getting dressed, and we sit on the sofa in the sitting room.

"What did you want to talk about?" I ask.

She blows out a breath, smiles, winces, then smiles and winces again.

"I'm not sure how to say this."

And right now, I'm not sure if I should be worried or what. She looks like whatever she's about to say might not be something I want to hear.

"Just blurt it out, baby," I encourage, taking her hand in mine.

She nods, then takes a deep breath before looking into my eyes.

"Xander," she begins.

"Yes."

"I, um, wow, this is harder than I thought. I mean, I'm worried about how you'll react."

"Now you're getting *me* worried. Just say it. We'll figure it out," I vow.

"Okay. Okay."

Another deep breath. Oh boy.

"It's like this, Xan. I kinda messed up."

My heart sinks into my stomach, and I swear it'd fall out my ass if I weren't sitting down.

"How? What's going on?"

She looks up, then looks back at me. "I'm pregnant."

It doesn't register. I'm expecting Tera to say she banged someone else or something. I mean, we had that agreement years back and after she said 'yes' that agreement changed. It's just been her and me. No one else. So... wait. What?

"Did you just say you're pregnant?" I ask, my voice actually squeaking.

She nods, biting her lower lip.

"Are you sure? I mean, did you see a doctor? Is this one okay? I know you had tests and they said things looked okay, but that doesn't mean they'll be okay. Holy shit. Really?"

She nods.

"A baby? Our baby. Holy shit!" I slide to the floor and hug her waist, resting my head on her abdomen. "I knew something was up. Your boobs are bigger, and you're curvier. Holy shit, Tera!"

She's laughing and crying at the same time.

"That's why you were sick. Have you been sick a lot? Do you know how far along you are?" I'm full of questions, and I can't stop kissing her stomach.

"I've been sick every day and usually around mid-afternoon, like now, and nighttime. It's brutal, X. *Brutal.*"

"Why didn't you tell me sooner? How far along did you say you were?"

She laughs. "I didn't say, but I'm just starting the second trimester, so four months. I wanted to wait to see if I made it through the first trimester. Miscarriages happen most often in the first trimester. I didn't want to tell you because I didn't want you to worry. I knew I was coming out here, but I had so many things to get organized before I did."

"Wow," I whisper. My heart is beating so hard. It feels so full. "Our baby is in there."

She nods. "Are you happy?"

I look up at her. "What? Baby, I'm fucking ecstatic! I'm just in the 'holy shit we're having a baby' and 'I'm so fucking excited I can't speak' stage."

"Oh, thank God. I was worried—"

"Baby. Never. I *love* you. I am so fucking happy right now I don't even have words, and you know that shit doesn't happen to me often."

"No, it certainly doesn't. I have an appointment with Dad after the new year."

I close my eyes as my heart swells even more. "I love that you're going to Dad. I—" I can't talk anymore. The tears fall. "I didn't know if we'd ever have a baby, and that would've been okay. If something happens and this doesn't work out, then that's what happens. I want you to know, Tera, you and me? We're more than enough—just so you know. In case. But, Jesus. We're having a baby!" I laugh.

"We are."

"You said you messed up. What did you mean?"

"I forgot to take my pills the days you came to visit. It wasn't on purpose. I'm so sorry, Xander."

"What? Stop. I know it wasn't on purpose. I kept you in bed that whole week. So, baby, it's not just on you. I remember that week. It was a damn fine week." Thinking about it is getting me horny. We fucked like rabbits, made love like it was the first time, and everything in between.

"Stop thinking about it," Tera teases. "We don't have time."

"Tera, there's always time for some Xander lovin'."

She laughs. "I'm sure the family is wondering if we're ever going to explain things to them."

"I'm sure they are, but holy fucking hell, Tera. Knowing you're pregnant with my baby and thinking of the week when I got you that way," I growl, my dick hard as stone. "I am so hard right now."

"I would help you with that, but I think if I tried, I'd be sick again. My nausea isn't so great right now," she offers.

"Don't even give it a thought. It can wait until later. And then again. I'm going to love you so good," I tell Tera, kissing her belly and up to her breasts. I cup them again. "I knew they were bigger. You're so fucking sexy."

I feel like a beast. There's some primal force, some man gene kicking in to where I feel powerful, more virile. Almost caveman-like.

"Holy shit! This is what Jesse felt when he went all growly on Lucy. I get it now. Man, I get it now. I feel like—I don't even know how to tell you. I really like knowing I knocked you up," I confess.

Tera rolls her eyes. "You would. Men, I swear. And while you like my boobs bigger, they're tender, so be gentle."

I nod. "I will. I promise. Man, this is... hell fucking yeah, Tera!" I shout, and she laughs. "Wait until we tell Dad. Wait until we tell Mr. and Mrs. M. They're going to go crazy."

"Well, Dad knows, since I asked him if it was okay to have him be my baby doctor," she admits.

"Damn. How come he always knows before me?" I whine.

"Aww, poor baby," she croons, teasing me.

"I want to know something first. Just once."

"Okay. How about this?"

I look up at her, feeling hopeful.

"If things work out how I hope they will, I'm moving out here to be with you. I want us to be a family," she tells me, looking nervous.

My heart stops, and I smile at her.

"There's nothing I want more."

Chapter Twenty-Three

Xander

"How mad did they look?" I ask Tera.

"I'm sure they're past the mad now and moved on to the disappointment and feelings of betrayal," she tells me.

"Gee, thanks a lot for putting that out there," I tease.

She shrugs. "I'm not going to sugar coat it for you. If I were Lucy or the other women who hadn't been let in on the fact that you were married, and you were *my* best friend, I'd be so hurt. They're your family, and Lucy's your best friend, right?"

I nod. "Yeah. I'm closest to Lucy and Jesse."

"Then, let's go fix this before it gets worse."

Worse. As with all things, it will get worse before it gets

better—but I'm keeping that to myself. I'm sure she knows it anyway, judging by her stiff posture.

I grab her hand again. "Let's go tackle this situation so I can tackle you—again." I wiggle my eyebrows and she snickers.

I stop where I keep my snacks and drinks, the kitchenette, and give my wife a bottle of ginger ale. "Glass? Ice?"

"Both, please. Light on the ice, though."

Let's hope the drama can be handled quickly and smoothly. I hate that I hurt their feelings. I hate that I hurt Lucy, of all people. It's time to explain what I can, for now. It's time to get my life back with Tera.

As we head down the stairs, we notice everyone's sitting in the holiday-decorated room where we all gather on special occasions, the only room that's big enough to hold all of us. And when I say everyone, I mean *everyone*. I squeeze Tera's hand gently to reassure her. I can feel her shaking with nerves. Looking down at the crowd, I can see how it could be intimidating.

"Tera!" Dad calls out. He walks over, and they hug.

I glance around the room. Jesse looks over, then winces in warning. I nod slightly. I figured it wasn't going to be good, at first. But I have my reasons for keeping this to myself—that being my wife's wishes. They'll have to understand, or they can go on being upset. Tera has to always come first—I learned that the hard way, we all did.

The second Dad lets loose of Tera, Lucy steps up.

She holds out her hand to Tera. "Hi. I'm Lucy, Jesse's wife."

Tera shakes Lucy's hand. "Tera, Xander's wife."

"Yeah," Lucy says, her tone leaving no question she's displeased. "I heard about that. It's great to meet you."

"Thanks," Tera answers. "You, too. Finally."

"Finally?" Lucy questions.

Tera nods. "I've heard so much about you—all of you."

Lucy taps her fingernail to her bottom lip. "Interesting. Xander hasn't been quite as forthcoming about you."

Tera winces. "I'm sorry about that. It's so complicated."

Lucy nods, then looks at me. "Xan, Xan, Xan. Looks like you got some 'splaining to do."

I knew this was coming. Tera and I will handle this like we're going to handle everything from here on out—together.

Chapter Twenty-Four

Tera

I STEEL MYSELF, mustering up the courage to face all of these people who mean so much to my husband. I can do this. *We* can do this.

Xander takes my hand and squeezes gently.

"Are all the kids napping?" Xan asks.

"Yeah, we put them down a little bit ago," Jesse answers.

"Shall we?" I ask Xander.

He nods, and we take a seat on some throw pillows adjacent to the fire. This gives everyone in the room a clear view of us.

"Hi," I begin. "I'm Tera."

Everyone introduces themselves and, oh boy, Lucy's parents and grandparents, Sera and her husband, Dad and Sandy, Meggie and Trace, Joey Russo—the movie star (I just watched a movie with him in it the other night!), Jace and Summer, Jesse and Lucy, Kennedy, Linc, Ethan, Ben and Nicole, Damian, Celeste, Ernesto, Joan, Nico, Bella, Emilio—all names I've heard but most of whom I've never met. Mama and Papa have gone to their living quarters behind the mansion. Guest house? That is so much more than a guest house.

"We'll start from the beginning," Xander tells them.

Xander tells them all of it. How he pushed me away and hated himself for it. How he missed out on those firsts with me. How they won the contest, and I was with them every step of the way, their biggest cheerleader, next to our dad.

"Hold up," Lucy says, frowning. "Keyboards. Linc played keyboards, didn't he?"

Xander nods, smiling.

"Stalkerrrr," Sera teases.

"He did. He also helped with the soundboards. The guy is a genius with the boards," Xander tells them.

He goes on to tell them about touring, spending time apart, asking me to marry him, how I refused the first time. He continues on with the second time he asked and how he had to leave for the tour a couple days later. He starts to explain about me being an artist, how I won that competition and went to LA…

Now, it's my turn.

"I'd won a contest and the gallery that held it had a showing for all of the finalists and winners. I should clarify. I paint. I'm an artist." Then, I tell them everything that happened. I don't go into great detail, I won't subject them to that. Lucy begins to cry. Others gasp. I hate telling this story, but at least I only have to do it once.

Xander wraps an arm around me when my voice begins to crack.

When I finish telling my part, Lucy walks over with a bottle of water and gives me a big hug.

"One day, we should talk, Tera. My story isn't nearly as tragic as yours, but I have one, too."

"I'd like that. Not to hear about your pain—"

She smiles softly and sniffles. "I know."

"That couldn't have been easy to share," Cage says.

I sniffle and wipe beneath my eyes.

"It wasn't," Linc answers for me. "She's had agoraphobia for nearly a decade, anxiety so bad she hyperventilates, and PTSD that can be debilitating."

"For those who don't know, agoraphobia is when a person is too afraid to leave their home because of what lies beyond those walls," Xander informs them. "It's the main reason Tera hasn't been with me—us. But, two years ago on Christmas, our anniversary, I asked her to say 'yes' and be with me. And she said yes. The entire time since, she's been fighting and slaying those demons. She's conquered the majority of them to get here. I hope to help her slay them all."

I smile at him, a tear escaping, as my husband tells his family everything about me, all while looking so proud.

"But, there's more. Between the attack and Xander asking me to come here, we had some very rough times, times where we weren't together. We both had a lot of growing up to do, and while we did it, we realized we didn't want to be without the other," I confess.

"That's so romantic," Meggie coos.

"Yeah, you'd think so," Jesse teases. "Not so much fun for a while there, and part of that is because of *all* of us. Not just Xan or Tera." Jesse confesses all, earning evil eyes and gasps from others around the room.

"Jesse James Kingston!" Mama Russo snaps.

"I know, Mama. I learned," Jesse defends.

"All of you boys," she huffs. "Thank goodness you grew into

good men."

I laugh when I hear "Yes, Mama" come from multiple male voices around the room.

"I should've videotaped that," Linc laughs.

Ethan shoves Linc. "You just wait."

Xander clears his throat. "I've loved Tera every day, together and apart, since I was eight years old and saw her on those monkey bars singing Alanis Morissette so off key, I'm surprised the dogs in the neighborhood weren't howling," I tell them with a smirk, remembering that day fondly.

I huff and playfully shove him. "So rude."

"After that, I went to her as often as I could, but it was too much for her. I hated it, but I started going to her every other month or something like that. We talked every day on the phone, Skype. About four years after that, Tera had an identity crisis."

"That wasn't just on me," I defend. "You remember the first time Xander was in the tabloids with one of the chicks that always hung around?"

"Yeah," Lucy says aloud, narrowing her eyes.

"Holy Hannah, I see where this is going," Nicole whispers.

"We had all made a promise," Jesse cuts in. "We promised Tera we'd keep Xander out of the tabloids and shit. We were doing really good, too, until that night."

"We hit number one for the first time," Ben defends.

"Oh, would you shut up with that already," Linc demands, exasperated with Ben.

"Still, we let our guard down and at the same time, let Tera down," Kennedy reasons.

"What we *didn't* know was that while we were celebrating after our concert, Tera was having a miscarriage," Ethan says softly.

Gasps. Then silence.

"Oh no. No, no, no. Who could blame her for having an

identity crisis after all of that?" Lucy asks, wiping her tears.

"Whoa," Summer says, Jace holding her close.

"Well, then," Meggie replies.

"Assholes," Nicole mutters and playfully slaps Ben.

"She wanted a break after that," Xan continues. "Not just from me coming to see her often, but cutting back on phone calls, as well. She wanted nothing to do with me. She pushed me away, and I blamed myself for letting her down. It wasn't until two years later when I finally had enough of being apart that I found out just how much I'd let her down."

"No one's judging you, Xan," Summer tells him.

"Maybe you should."

"No," she replies. "We weren't there. I can only imagine."

He nods. "It fucking sucked. The photos came out and were every fucking where. They'd been trying for years to get dirt on us, you know? They'd heard rumors, but never had there been any photos or anything."

"I remember that," Lucy says. "They plastered those images everywhere, and they made it look so nasty."

"They sure did, and that... that is what my troubled wife sees the day after she loses our baby. She turns on the TV for her usual morning programs, and there it is. Ethan went to her before the rest of us even knew what was going on. I tried calling, but no one answered. I knew. I knew. The rules were broken, even if it wasn't my fault. I'd gotten careless. I knew better, but I was partying with the other guys. Thing is, they were single. I was married."

"What was in the photos?" Nicole asks.

"I wasn't doing anything but sitting on a sofa, some chick next to me, drinks in everyone's hands. Jesse... never mind that," Xander says, looking at Lucy.

She makes a face. "I saw them. Jesse had two chicks on his lap. One was looking for his tonsils with her tongue while he had his hand beneath the other's skirt. Ben, uh…"

Nicole snorts. "Go on. I know who and what he was before I married him."

"You sure?" Lucy asks.

"Yeah. It's fine."

"Well, Ben was getting blown right there. Kennedy had his guitar. Ethan was there but holding a soda can, that I remember," Lucy concludes.

"I didn't even notice that chick. I was too fucked up. Hell, I was too fucked up to get it up that night. So, while the pictures damned me, I wasn't doing anything wrong aside from drinking my weight in tequila."

Xan begins talking about our time apart. Me doing friends-with-benefits with Dante and him doing his thing.

"I mean, she's my wife, right? I trusted her, even when I was a fucking asshole out there getting blown when I felt the need to get off. But, Christ, believe me when I say, it's not like you think. I wasn't like Jesse. I spent a lot of time with my hand and a bottle of Jergens," Xander tells them.

Summer snorts.

I shake my head. "I didn't want to see him. I buried myself in my paintings. I only used Dante whenever I wanted to get off. It was nothing but sex. Maybe a little bit of a weapon to hurt Xander in return for him parading around with all those… well. It was a very ugly time for both of us."

"How did you get through it?" Meggie asks.

"You mean, how did we resolve things?" I ask.

"Yeah," Meggie answers.

I smirk, and Xander chuckles.

"It certainly wasn't easy," he begins. "I'd had enough. Just… enough. I didn't want to be without her anymore. So, I hopped the next flight with a really shitty plan. The next morning, I went to her place with a cup of coffee."

Sera snorts. "Are you serious? Did that work?"

I snicker. "Um… no."

Sera winks and gives me a thumb's up.

"She opened the door a crack, looked at me, looked at the coffee I was offering, and then shut the door in my face," Xan explains. "This for days! I switched tactics and brought her favorite flowers."

"Dude," Linc says.

"Yeah, that didn't work so well, either. Nothing worked. Then we had a teleconference one day, and Cage Dude was on the line. I needed help, and these guys weren't giving it to me. So, I asked the boss man," Xander explains.

"I didn't know that," I say.

Cage merely nods in response.

"And what did my brilliant husband tell you to do?" Sera asks.

"He told me she didn't want things. She didn't *want* anything. She *needed* to be told she was loved. So, that's what I did."

"Did that work?" Lucy asks.

"Not the first time," I answer.

"The second?" she asks.

"Well, that didn't work out the way I expected it to," I answer. "You see, I'd done so much thinking when Xan walked up those stairs, knocked on my door, blurted out 'I love you', then walked away. I knew I didn't want him to walk away again. But the next day, he didn't show up at the time he usually did. I waited and waited. When he didn't show, I started to panic and cry. I don't remember how late he was that day. All I remember is the knock and not being able to open the locks fast enough. I was so afraid he'd disappear before I could open the door," I tell them, getting lost in the memory.

"What happened when you opened the door?" Jace asks, rapt with attention.

I smile. "I opened the door, and Xan was on his knees. He told me he loved me and I couldn't stop crying. I dropped to my knees with him, and he kept asking what was wrong," I laugh a little at the memory.

"She told me she thought I wasn't going to show up. After all that time, she should have known better," Xander adds.

I look at him, love shining in his eyes, and I know I made the right choice coming here. He is everything to me. He is my love, my light, my *life*. There's no going back now.

"And they lived happily ever after?" Meggie prods.

Xan and I grin at one another. "After the fight," we say together.

"Fight?" Lucy asks.

"We couldn't be together unless we worked things out. It was all going smoothly and then…" Xander tells them.

"Snap!" I finish. "We called the guys, so I didn't have to repeat things more than once. There was no way I could've gone through that twice."

"You didn't have enough glassware on your shelves to make it twice," Linc adds.

"Uh," I hedge. "Let's just say, words flew, as well as an entire shelf of knick-knacks, a vase, and a few other breakable things."

"Oh, I really, really like her," Meggie declares.

Trace chuckles. She must be a handful. But it looks like he can handle her just fine.

"Then, we talked things out," Jesse continues. "It wasn't easy. I felt like the biggest piece of shit."

"One of the worst days of my life," Kennedy adds.

"Yeah," Ethan murmurs.

"Then, we hung up, her and Xan worked their shit out, and we showed up the next day. We worked hard to get back to the place we were before, but I think it's stronger now," Ben deduces.

I nod. "I'd have to agree."

"And you two? How did that work?" Lucy asks.

I sigh. "We saw one another as much as we could, but I just wasn't ready to be in the spotlight of *Falling Down* and my rockstar husband. I couldn't leave the apartment."

"I promised to never pressure her, and I didn't. Not until all you fuckers started getting married off. I wanted that. I wanted Tera with me, so Christmas two years ago, I asked her to say yes," Xander tells them.

I nod. "He did. I knew what he meant without him having to ask any more than that. And I knew my answer was yes before I replied. I was ready. But it took me this long to get here. I had *a lot* of therapy, intensive therapy, for the last two years. It took thirteen months before I would step outside of my apartment. Fourteen months until I made it to the bottom of the stairs. With each week and month that passed, I made more progress. I didn't tell Xander too much about it. Just that I was getting there. I sent him a photo of me standing outside, but that's as much information as he got. I wanted to surprise him—today. On Christmas—our anniversary."

"And I was surprised. In more ways than one," he begins, then looks at me to make sure it's okay. I blink and nod slightly.

"Oh," Lucy gasps.

Xander laughs. "We're having a baby!"

"I knew it. I just knew it when you walked in today," Summer begins. "I don't know how I knew, but I did. I told Jace, and he told me I was crazy." She pokes him. "Not so crazy now, am I?"

"That's not the reason I came, though. I had this planned before I even knew…"

"Oh, Tera. We know that," Lucy begins, then comes over and hugs me again. "We *know*. We can see it."

"You'd have to be blind not to," Mama Russo agrees.

"Does this mean you all forgive me?" Xander asks.

Lucy scoffs. "I want to be mad at you. I *should* be mad at you.

But with a story like yours, how can I? You were true to Tera." Lucy looks around, then lands on Jesse. "All of you were. I respect that, even if it does sting I didn't know."

"I'm sorry, Cupcake. You know I'd have told you..."

"I know. I do. I get it—and I'll get past the hurt, too. I promise," Lucy tells her husband, giving him a hug this time.

"Looks like you fuckers dodged a bullet," Linc teases.

"Lincoln Ramirez! You will watch your language," Mama Russo chastises.

"Yes, ma'am," he agrees, looking sheepish.

The entire room bursts into laughter.

"My big, tattooed, underground fighting brother cowers to this lovely Italian lady. Please tell me someone got that on film," I joke.

Ethan smirks. "Oh, I got it. I knew he was just biding his time before he cursed and I knew Mama R was gonna get him for it."

"You could've warned me," Linc tells Ethan.

"Hell no! We didn't get a warning," Xander tells Linc.

"Yeah, whatever," Lincoln mumbles, sounding much like the little boy who got scolded in school.

"Aww, poor baby," I croon.

"Yeah, yeah," he replies.

Lucy walks up and smiles at Xander and me.

"He's my best friend," she begins. "I hope you'll be okay with that. I don't think I could live in a world where he's not my best friend."

Tears glisten in her eyes, and she's so genuine, I start to tear up, as well.

"Of course it's okay. Xander told me everything—*everything*. I get it, and I want to thank you, Lucy. I want to thank you for being there for him. For making him smile and laugh even when life wasn't so easy," I tell her. "I certainly don't want that to stop. Xander laughing is the best sound in the world."

She laughs with me. "It certainly is."

Jesse walks over to me and hugs me close. "Thank you, Tera. I know that wasn't easy."

"It was easier than I thought it would be," I tell him honestly.

Jesse nods. "I'd give them anything they asked for."

It's my turn to nod. "Me too. How could we not, when they've given us the world?"

Chapter Twenty-Five

Tera

New Year's Eve

WE HAVE A charity gala to attend in Vegas. This will be a test to my anxiety, but I think I'll be okay. Cage insisted on security, and that makes me feel better. At least I didn't have to ask for it.

We take the private jet to Las Vegas, and I'm very impressed with Falling Down's success. I guess I never really thought about how much they made. While I have access to Xander's money and he has access to mine, I never looked at his account. I don't know if he's ever looked at mine, but I've done well for myself. I take pride in that.

We get ready in our rooms at the MGM Grand. The gala will be downstairs, as well as an MMA fight that's being held beforehand.

I'm wearing a lace, jade, one shoulder long-sleeve, floor-length dress with a slit up one leg and scalloped detail throughout. When Lucy's stylists came in to help with my hair and makeup, I made sure to tell them that standing too close behind me was a no-go. I still, to this day, can't stand the feel of a stranger's breath on the back of my neck. It sends me into a full-on panic attack, and it's so not pretty.

We're all glammed up, and sitting ringside when the announcer broadcasts the first fighter.

"Johnny 'The Bone Crusher' Rodriiii-gueeeeez!"

The crowd erupts and so does the music.

Falling Down. I've heard them on the radio, on my iPod, and even on TV, but I haven't seen them live since before they hit number one.

It's all drums and cheers and riffs and chaos—and then it's Jesse Kingston. He's in his element up there with his aviators on, jeans, and black Metallica t-shirt. And that voice of his—I'm woman enough to admit it's sexy as hell when he growls, as he is known to do. The crowd screams—mostly female screams are what I hear.

I know who you are
I know where you come from
I know where you've been
I'm gonna stop you from where you're goin'

I'm going to break you
I'm going to crush you
I'm going to rape you

I'm going to annihilate you
You won't see me comin'
I'm stalking my prey
You won't see me comin'
I'm the bone crusher, hey!

You think you know me
You think I care
You think you're the shit
You think I'm fuckin' scared

Dream on, you won't rip me
Walk on, you don't grip me
Go on and think what you want
I'm comin' for you

I'm going to break you
I'm going to crush you
I'm going to annihilate you
I'm going to conquer you

I'm!
Going!
To crush!
Yooooou!

Yeah, I'm gonna crush you
I'm gonna grind you down
I'm gonna crush you
I'm gonna crush you

Crush! You!

Cheers go up for the band and the fighter.

I couldn't help but cringe at the word *rape*. Just hearing the word nearly sends me into a spiral, but with Lucy dancing and holding onto my arm, I'm anchored pretty tightly to reality. *Just breathe, Tera. Just Breathe.*

"Wow. That was really intense," Sera mutters.

"I am so hot for my husband right now," Lucy tells her, and Sera laughs.

They continue chattering for a few minutes, and I take in all the people in their formal attire, the lone fighter in the ring waiting for his opponent, and Falling Down exiting the stage set up in the far right corner.

Gavin "The Ripper" Jones enters to In This Moment's Adrenalize. This is one band I'm not a fan of, but I cheer anyway.

I take in the fighters. One's leaner than the other but more defined.

Oh, the muscles on these men. Delicious. I now understand why strange women lust after my brother.

"This is going to get bloody, I think," Lucy tells me.

"I think so, too."

Lucy's been really welcoming to me since I've arrived on their doorstep. I wouldn't have blamed her if she would have been rude or didn't talk to me much at all. I would have understood, seeing how close she and Xander are.

Watching him with those babies is lovely. I can't wait to see him with ours.

"That was disgusting," I tell Lucy when "The Ripper" delivers a blow to his opponent that sends blood and spit flying from his mouth.

"Just, ick," Lucy replies. "Let's ignore the blood and spit and focus on the rippling muscles."

I sigh, taking in said muscles. "Yes, let's."

Looking past the blood didn't work out too well.

"I'm going to find Jesse. Hopefully, he can fuck that image out of my head," Lucy says with a shudder.

I nod. "Just… yuck."

"Oh, come on," Sera teases. "Didn't you look past the blood and see those hot male specimens?"

"Who could see past the blood?" I squeak, my stomach queasy, and it has nothing to do with the baby.

I hear Sera laugh as we walk away, and I don't even care.

"Sera's a hardass," Lucy tells me.

"I got that. Xander told me a lot about everyone." I wipe my brow and feel beads of sweat. "Oh, wow. I really don't feel well." The room begins to spin a little.

Lucy grabs my arm. "Are you okay?" She calls one of the security guards over. "I don't know where Xander is, but Tera's feeling unwell. We need to get her up to the room before she passes out."

"I think that's a good idea," I reply. The world tilts, and it's then I realize Linc is standing there, lifting me into his arms.

"Little sister, did you eat today? Have you been drinking enough?"

"I did, and I have. I think maybe the heels are too much," I mutter, irritated because these are one of my favorite pair of Jimmy Choos. Black, strappy sandals with a four-inch heel.

Linc looks at my feet, then shakes his head. "Tera."

"Shut up," I whine as the elevator doors open.

By the time we get to the room, Xander is there, waiting for us.

"Are you okay?" Xander asks. He's looking frantic.

"I'm okay," I reassure him. Linc sets me down on the sofa, and I take a sip from the water bottle Ethan passes me. He blots my brow with a cold cloth.

"This might ruin your makeup, but you look so pale, Tera," Ethan explains.

"I'm sorry to worry everyone."

"Don't be sorry," Lucy tells me. "It could have been the heels, but I bet all that blood didn't help."

I groan. "No, that definitely did not help."

"If you're not up for going down for dinner, we can order in," Xander tells me, coming to sit next to me, pulling me onto his lap.

"I just need a minute to recover. Who knew pregnancy could be so trying?" I ask no one in particular.

"Me," Lucy replies, raising her hand. "I have a book you need to read. It tells you about all the things going on in your body right now, all the changes—and there are a lot."

"I don't know how you did it with four," I admire.

Lucy laughs humorlessly. "It sucked. Sucked with a capital S. It was summer and I was as big as a house. I kept tipping over."

Linc chuckles and Jesse punches him. "Dude. Really not funny. Can you imagine over 13 pounds of babies in that little woman's belly?"

Linc sobers quickly, then drops to his knees and bows his top half to the floor. "I bow to your greatness. No joke."

Jesse lifts a brow at me. "What if there's more than one in there?"

I look to where Jesse's pointing at my belly.

"Uh… that better not happen," I say aloud. "No. That will not happen." I give Xander the evils.

"Hey, if there's more than one in there it's not my fault your eggs like my swimmers," he defends.

"You suck," I reply.

Linc laughs. "I have a comeback for that, but I don't dare."

"Smart man. You're learning," Jesse praises.

"I'm going to use the restroom. Then I think I'm okay to go down. I'm hungry."

"You're always hungry," Lincoln calls after me. I keep walking as I flip him the bird over my shoulder.

Lucy laughs. "I really, really like her."

"Me too," Xander replies as I close the door.

Chapter Twenty-Six

Xander

THE GALA IS super classy, all black and white. Reminds me of how CFD used to be when we had the black and white tiled floor—before Jesse went all Papa Bear and had carpet put in with about two inches of foam padding. Just in case one of the kids fell. At first, I thought he was overdoing it. Then they started to walk—the K-Quads, and that changed everything.

We find our table and somehow, they managed to squeeze all eleven of us onto one table. Sera and Cage, Lucy and Jesse, Tera and me, Ben and Nicole, Kennedy, Ethan, and Linc.

Tera and Lucy coo about the dim lighting with the white fairy lights that surround the edges of the room.

"It's so romantic," Lucy adds.

"I'm proud to be here tonight," I say out loud. "Sponsoring such a great charity, something that hits close to home—well, it's a good choice."

I think of Nicole and Linc, as well. Both suffered from leukemia and both needed financial help to get them through. Organizations like St. Jude's Children's Network are ones I support and donate to on a regular basis.

"What's on your mind, Fee?" Cage asks.

Sera looks up at him. "It pisses me off that there isn't a cure."

He nods.

"If only they didn't have to go through what they do. If only it were as simple to cure as the common cold," Sera murmurs, a tear slipping free.

Cage reaches up and wipes it away with his thumb. "Fee."

I look away, their conversation is a private one, an intimate one I don't want to intrude on.

"I don't think you all know, but Nicole's not the only one who battled the big C," I begin. "Linc had a brief battle with leukemia, as well. It wasn't pretty, but he kicked its ass just like you did, Coley."

Nicole smiles. "I'm so glad you did, Linc."

"Ditto. Some day we can share war stories," Linc replies.

"I'm going to hold you to that."

Dinner is served.

Jesse bites into his lamb and I note Sera watching him.

"Baaaaah," Sera voices.

He looks up, brows furrowed.

"Baaaaah." She does it again, and I'm trying hard not to laugh. I nudge Tera with my elbow and she snickers.

Jesse raises one of his brows as he chews thoughtfully.

"Mary's missing her little lamb," I say and Sera nods.

"Totally is because Jesse's eating it! Baaaaah!" Sera adds.

"What about you, over there? You're eating Nemo. Or maybe

it's Dori. Maybe it's Nemo's dad?" Jesse mocks.

"Whoever it was should have just kept swimming and they wouldn't be on my plate," Sera snarks and we all crack up.

"And Mary should have taken the key and locked her up and the lamb wouldn't be on my plate," Jesse retorts.

Sera shakes her head and snickers. "That's London Bridge, but I'll give it to you. Well done, brother-in-law. Well done."

Jesse fakes a bow, still sitting. "Thank you. I'll be here all week. Not really, but… really, how does that go? Mary had a little lamb?" He forks a piece of meat into his mouth and Sera visibly shudders and Tera gets pale.

"Nasty."

"You should know your nursery rhymes by now, Kingston. What the fuck?" I taunt.

"There are way too fucking many. You've seen that stack of books in the baby room. No way can I remember that shit," Jesse replies.

"Yet you can remember your locker combination from freshman year in high school," I scoff.

"Damn straight. It's 34-15-12."

"Freak," Kennedy mutters.

I lean over and whisper to Lucy. "Hey, we going Elvis hunting later?"

Lucy nods enthusiastically. "I was hoping you would ask. Tera's coming, too, right?"

Tera smirks. "I wouldn't miss this for anything."

"It's going to be so great."

"Uh-oh," Sera mutters and Jesse sighs.

Kennedy laughs. "They're going Elvis hunting again."

"And taking Tera with them," Ethan announces, brows raised.

"Did you think I'd just sit here when there's a mission to be accomplished?" Tera asks.

Sera looks to Lucy. "Sister of mine, I'm turning my phone off and getting my kink on with Batman tonight, so if you need bail money, you're gonna have to call someone else."

Lucy nods. "Noted. Did that one Elvis really get a restraining order?"

Sera snickers.

Cage sighs. "Please avoid that Elvis, Lucy. My phone will be off, as well, and I'd hate to wake up to a shit storm tomorrow morning."

Lucy smirks. "I make no promises."

Cage sighs again.

"It's just a little Xananigans," Tera declares proudly.

"Oh hell," Ethan mutters. "She's got a word for it."

I grin proudly and throw my arm around Tera and give her a smacking kiss. "She participates. Of course, she's going to have a word for it. Xananigans," I repeat. "I like it."

Cage scrubs a hand over his face and shakes his head, chuckling as he does.

Sera smirks and elbows Cage gently. "Are you wondering how this has become your life?"

Now he laughs. "Close enough."

"Imagine how boring it'd be without this," Sera tells him, looking around the table.

Cage nods. "Boring… or peaceful?"

Sera shrugs. "Same diff."

"I suppose," he mutters.

"Admit it, Cage Dude. You love me," I tease.

"I wouldn't go that far," Cage replies.

"I'm wounded. Deeply, deeply wounded," I retort, feigning sadness.

Cage sits there, the only sign of his amusement is the tiny lift of one of the corners of his mouth. "You'll recover."

Sera whispers something to Cage and he gets a look on his face he only gets when Sera's around.

"If you'll excuse us," Cage addresses.

"Oh, yeah! Sera and Batman sexy time!" I call out. Everyone joins in. There are wolf whistles and cat calls until they exit the ballroom.

I laugh. "That was awesome."

"Imagine how fun Elvis hunting is going to be!" Lucy replies.

Indeed.

Elvis hunting didn't go as planned. Poor Lucy's sad. Someone rained on the Elvis parade last night and if I'd have had more liquor in me, I'd have likely punched them in the face. As it was, Linc lifted this Elvis up by his gold lamé lapels and gave him a good, hard shake. I swear we heard his teeth rattle. It seems no one likes to see an upset Lucy.

We went back to the hotel, hung out in the suite, and Lucy got completely shitfaced. Drunk Lucy is hilarious—unless someone fucks up her plans, and that asshole Elvis did just that.

"Do you think Lucy's still upset?" Tera asks as we finish getting dressed to go down for breakfast.

"Yeah, I'm sure she is. I'm fucking bummed about it myself. Why'd that fuckface have to ruin our fun?" I whine.

"Aww, my poor baby," Tera croons, hugging me.

"It's just, we have so much fun when we go Elvis hunting," I whine some more.

"He's not really dead. That article was in the Enquirer, for fuck's sake. Total bullshit. And there is *no way* Elvis looks like that. He looked horrible. Elvis is too handsome to look that shitty."

"Valid point," I reply.

"We'll just have to come back and avoid that lousy Elvis. I did go and tell the casino manager what a dick he was. I think he got fired," Tera tells me happily.

"Good. He was a total dick to Luce."

"He wasn't any better to you."

I let out a sigh. "No, but I can handle shit like that. Lucy's too soft-hearted."

"I'll talk to her at breakfast. Let's go down. I'm hungry."

"Woman, pregnancy makes you hungry all the time—for both food and sex," I remind her.

"Are you seriously complaining?"

"Hell no!"

She laughs. "I didn't think so."

Chapter Twenty-Seven

Tera

WE MAKE OUR way to the buffet and, oh my God, am I hungry. Bacon. Bacon, bacon, and more bacon. French toast with strawberries and whipped cream. Scrambled eggs. Hash browns. I fill a bowl with a mixture of fruits.

"Uh," Xander begins, looking at my overflowing plate with raised brows.

"Yes?" I ask, not even a little ashamed. I'm damn hungry. There's a baby growing in there, and he or she is hungry, too.

"Do you want coffee? Juice?"

"Decaf coffee with creamer," I begin.

"Of course."

"Apple juice would be perfect. Lots of apple juice," I tell him, stuffing a piece of bacon in my mouth.

Xander grins, those beautiful white teeth showing, his dimples winking, and I sigh blissfully.

"I love you, Xan."

His eyes go soft. "I love you, Tera." He kisses my lips. "I'll get your beverages, babe."

"Thanks," I reply, eating more bacon.

"Damn it, Tera," Linc bitches, "you didn't take the whole thing of bacon, did you?"

"Screw you. If I did, I wouldn't share. Not with that tone," I reply, lifting my nose to snub him. "That'll teach you to do tequila shots, you freaking lightweight."

"I'm not a lightweight," he defends.

"Lies. I don't ever drink, but even I can outdrink you," I remind him.

"Yeah, well."

His go-to reply when he's proven wrong.

Ethan chuckles, then groans and grabs his head.

"I have some pain reliever if you want some for your hangover headache," I offer to Ethan.

"You, Tera, are a goddess. I bow at your feet. I will forever be your servant," Ethan teases, coming over and accepting the tablets, taking a couple more for Linc.

"Get away from my wife, you lech," Xan teases.

Sera and Cage come walking up. Sera looks at Lucy then at Xander questioningly.

Xander makes a sign of the cross. "Elvis is dead."

"What?" Sera asks.

Xan nods. "We went to Denny's last night looking for Skinny Elvis, the one who married Jesse and Lucy. He wasn't there but the one who was told us there was an article in the newspaper that Elvis was found dead under one of the overpasses near LA."

"I'm sure it was bullshit," Sera placates.

I shake my head. "There was a photo."

"A photo?"

Kennedy's grinning as he bites into his strip of bacon and Ethan's smirking. Ben and Nicole both turn away.

"Yes, a photo," Lucy says vehemently. She pounds a fist on the table. Jesse wraps his arm around her, biting his lip, trying not to laugh. "There was no mistaking it was him. It was a photo of him at the age he would be now."

Cage coughs into his coffee.

"I'm so sorry, Luce," Sera says, when in reality I can tell she wants to laugh.

Lucy nods, sniffling again. "I just wanted to meet him."

"I know, baby," Jesse replies, rubbing her arm with his hand, pulling her closer to his side.

"Do you think he died happy?" Xan asks.

Cage opens his mouth to reply, but Sera kicks his foot under the table. Kennedy snickers and Ethan grins. Ben and Nicole still have their backs toward us, but I see their shoulders shaking with laughter.

"I'm sure he died happier than he would have had he died by overdosing on the toilet," Sera answers.

"He was homeless," Lucy adds.

Sera sighs. "Homeless or not, I'm sure he lived a happy life, Luce."

Lucy nods. "We should go to Graceland sometime. Pay our respects to his memory."

"Yes. Let's do that soon," Xan agrees. I nod along.

"We've got some gigs lined up in Memphis and Nashville next month. That'd be a good time," Cage offers.

Lucy and Jesse are up at the buffet and Lucy looks miserable.

"I have a plan," I whisper to Xan.

He nods. "I'm in."

Lucy sits across from me and Jesse across from Xander at the long table Lincoln, Kennedy, and Ethan have chosen for us. Sera and Cage are sitting adjacent to Jesse.

"Lucy," I begin.

She looks up, despondent and bleak.

"Your mission, should you choose to accept it, is to come back to Vegas with all of us and go on the true Elvis hunting mission we got cheated out of by that lying Fat Elvis bastard," I challenge.

"But he's dead."

I scoff. "You really think Elvis would look that shitty? Dead, alive; old, young? Please. He's Elvis."

Lucy perks up. "That's right. Even when he got fat, he was handsome. That lying bastard." She pounds the table again.

"Luce," Xander begins. "It was the Enquirer. Of all the rags out there, that one is the worst. Remember the alien boy? All the UFO bullshit?"

She nods more enthusiastically now. Beside her, Jesse grins and winks at me.

"I remember that!" she shouts, then looks around. "Oops. I didn't mean to shout, I was just so excited."

"Who isn't?" I reply. "This is our mission."

"You're going to have to hold off on that for a month or so," Cage tells me.

"Oh?" I ask, devouring more bacon.

Cage looks around the table. "I got a call this morning. Falling Down and Blush are requested to perform at four charity concerts. There's one in Nashville, as I mentioned earlier."

"When?" Jesse asks.

"One each Saturday for the next month."

Jesse nods, as do the Falling Down members.

"I'll need to talk to the rest of the band. I don't know what Jace,

Meggie, or Trace have planned since this is such short notice," Lucy explains to Cage.

He nods. "I figured as much. I need to know asap."

"I'll make the calls after breakfast," Lucy agrees.

"Perfect." Cage turns his attention to me. "How would you feel about going with us, Tera?"

I look at Xander, who's watching me. "This is what I'm afraid of most. I'm afraid if I get there, to the venue, and you're out there performing, and the crowd backstage gets rowdy, or even the audience, that I'll have an anxiety attack. I need to be extra careful since I'm pregnant and unable to take any of the medications."

"We always have security. I mean, Damian's there. I'm sure he'd be happy to escort you and ensure your safety," Xander answers.

I nod. "I'm just afraid, and I don't want you to worry about me while you're up there playing for the crowd."

"We'll work this out," Cage assures me. "I can have as many men protecting you as you need to feel safe. No number is too big."

"Anything you need, Tera," Sera begins, "it's yours."

I bite my lip. I feel stupid. I want at least four, but is that overkill? Will they think I'm a silly and crazy chick?

"Stop," Lucy commands. "No one judges anyone in this family. No one."

"Was it that obvious?" I ask.

She nods. "It was. When Sera says 'anything you need', that's precisely what we all mean. I can't even imagine how difficult this is for you without your medications."

She looks down at my wrist, where I'm snapping my anxiety wristband. I stop and cover the band with my other hand.

"Please, don't, Tera. Don't be embarrassed. Don't feel ashamed. Not with us. You don't with the guys, right?" Lucy asks.

"Right," I reply.

"We're just an extension of them. We genuinely care about you.

You are our family." Lucy grasps my hand and squeezes gently. "I promise you. No one will ever judge you."

"Never," Sera assures me. "That's not how this family works."

Tears fill my eyes. They've accepted me as family. "Just like that?"

Jesse nods. "Just like that."

I sniffle and nod. My gaze slides back to Lucy. "Thank you." I look over to Sera and Cage. "All of you."

Xander wipes his eyes. "Best family ever."

I nod and kiss him softly. "Thank you for letting me be a part of it."

He pulls me to him and hugs me fiercely. "You will always be my family, Tera. You always have been. Since day one."

I nod. "I know. I know."

Lucy lets out a sob. "This… oh, my heart is so happy right now."

"Cupcake," Jesse murmurs, then kisses her cheek. "Such a good heart."

I lean out of Xander's embrace and slap his hand as he tries to steal a piece of bacon.

"Don't even. I will stab your hand with my fork," I warn.

"Dude," Jesse mutters. "Don't mess with a pregnant woman's food."

"But it's bacon, and bacon is meat candy. I want some," Xander tells me.

I point my fork to the buffet. "Go get some, then. I meant it when I said I'd stab you with this fork."

"Pregnancy has made you violent," Xander teases.

"And it only gets worse from here," Ben replies.

When did he get here? And Coley.

Dad and Sandy come walking up.

"Dad?" I question, standing up to give him a hug, then Sandy.

"What are you doing here?" I look between him and Sandy, and they're both smiling.

"We got married," Sandy blurts out, and Dad laughs.

"That was not part of the plan."

She snickers. "Who needs a plan?"

He kisses her forehead.

"Well, it's about damn time," Lincoln bellows. "Hey, everyone! Our dad and Sandy got married... finally... after twenty-plus years!"

The entire restaurant erupts into cheers and applause.

"Dad, you stud," Xander calls out, hugging him and slapping him on the back in the way guys do. Then he looks to Sandy. "Mom, gimme some sugar."

I start laughing. I can't stop, either. The look on Sandy's face is priceless. One of resignation and mirth. She hugs Xander back and kisses his cheek.

"This is just too good," Jesse exclaims, laughing with me.

"He's going to start calling her mommy and shit," Linc declares.

"I can already see it," I agree. "Are you staying here a while for a honeymoon?"

Dad shakes his head. "Nope. I've got two weeks of work, then Sandy and I are going to Paris for ten days."

"Oh, Paris is so lovely," Lucy replies.

One day, I'll get there. One day, I'll go to all the places I've dreamed of going. But for now, I'm enjoying this dream that's come true. A big family, the man of my dreams as my husband, and our baby growing inside me. It's a dream I hope never ends.

Chapter Twenty-Eight

Tera

Three days later...

"I DIDN'T KNOW you had nannies," I tell Lucy.

"We had to. We're working on new albums, both bands, so that means long hours and someone needs to help out with the babies," she explains.

"I see. How did you find them?"

"My agent asked around to some very good friends of hers. I could've asked Cage, but he'd have likely given us one of the Russo enforcers," she jokes.

"About that."

She raises her brows.

"Is your family really the Italian mafia?"

She nods. "Yep. I've accepted it for what it is."

"Which is?"

Lucy pours some milk into a sippy cup. "They buy and sell goods—illegal, of course. Weapons mostly. I'm not involved, at all. It's just not something I can stomach. Sera, on the other hand, she's got a taste for blood."

"Really," I probe.

"Oh, yes." Lucy explains about the death of Sera's parents, which Xander gave me the cliff notes of.

"Holy shit. I think I'd have a taste for it, too, if I were her. She's good with a gun, you said?"

Lucy laughs. "She could hit a bullseye blindfolded. I'm not kidding. And with her mixed martial arts training, she's a lethal weapon."

I whistle. "Remind me never to piss her off."

"No worries there. She doesn't hurt family unless they become traitors. Then all bets are off."

I nod. "That won't be a problem. How does Cage feel about her being so active in the family?"

Lucy shrugs as she fills another cup. "He doesn't like it, but Sera's her own person and he knows that. He'd never tell her what she could and couldn't do. Our grandpa, Giovanni, he's in charge of what we call La Famiglia or Russo Famiglia. He doesn't like women being involved in the business, but the times they are a'changing, and he's found out there is no sexism in business anymore."

"Wait. I thought women weren't allowed?" I am so ignorant when it comes to this stuff.

"Not anymore. There are some women in charge of 'families'. While the old-school families still hold true to the no-women rule, many now allow anyone who wants to and can pass all the necessary challenges, to participate in the family," Lucy explains.

"So, people like Sera, who are trained, who can shoot and defend themselves."

"Exactly. Not everyone in the family has what it takes to be part of the business. I don't have the blood thirst for it. Don't get me wrong, I could kill someone if I needed to. I've been trained in hand-to-hand combat as well as knives and guns. But I choose not to. I don't think I could live with myself if I killed someone just because I was ordered to, just because they had the wrong last name, you know?"

"That happens?"

"More than I care to admit knowing about."

"Wow. Xander mentioned things, but I had no idea." I'm not sure how I feel about that.

"This can't be repeated."

I nod my agreement.

"Cage is my grandfather's second."

I can't hide my surprise. I knew he had involvement, I just didn't know...

"I didn't expect that."

Lucy nods. "No one does. He's a gentle man to those he loves. To his enemies, he's ruthless."

"That's a little unnerving," I admit.

"I wouldn't let it get to you. Cage is a good man. He'd do anything for family—and you're family now," she reminds me.

So. I'm part of the "family". I never even thought about that. That means my baby is, too.

"Are we safe?" I ask.

"Oh, yes. Safer than any average Joe on the street. Our security is top notch and, mostly, no one messes with us," she tells me with a wink.

"I'm guessing they know better."

"You got it. Now, go finish packing. This is going to be a fun weekend. Chicago! Our home town!"

I nod. I'm not so excited about Chicago. There's nothing left for me there. All of my family and friends have moved on.

I head toward our suite when the doorbell rings. I don't see anyone around, so I detour and yell out, "I got it!"

I open the door and there stands Carter Winters!

"Yeah, you sure do got it, baby!" he bellows, then lifts me into a hug, spinning me around. I squeal in surprise.

"Oh my God! What are you doing here?" I ask.

"You invited me. That open invitation, remember?" he asks, wiggling his eyebrows.

I hear footsteps behind me and I laugh while Carter spins me again.

"What the hell is going on here?" Xander yells as he sprints down the stairs. "Jesus, is that Carter fucking Winters in my house? What the hell are you doing in my house, Winters?"

I laugh into Carter's neck. "He's going to feel like an asshole in about two minutes."

Carter nods.

"I came to see Tera."

"Oh really. That's interesting," Xander says, giving me the squinty eye. I laugh and he squints his eyes even more. "Is something funny, *wife*?"

I laugh again. "Yes, as a matter of fact."

"What's funny?" he bites out.

I see Linc grinning, Ethan smirking, Kennedy just waiting, Jesse and Lucy eating popcorn. Ben and Nicole are standing there, each holding an adorable little dog. I want one!

"You're going to feel really silly in about ten seconds," I tell him.

"Why's that?"

I can hear her heels on the steps.

"Five, four, three, two, one…"

"What's shakin', fellas and ladies!" Shea yells out.

Xander looks confused and I snicker. It's mean, but he did this to himself.

"I repeat, what the hell is going on here?" Xan yells again.

"Jesus, we heard you the first time," Carter answers.

"Watch yourself, Winters," Xander tells him as he points.

Shea laughs. "This is so amusing. I'd let it go on, but he looks so sad standing there. Poor, lost Xander—who brought this on himself. This will teach you to be nice to house guests."

"Um, Xan," I begin, walking over to where he's standing, legs apart, arms folded across his chest—it's an aggressive stance and it's so un-Xander-like.

"Woman, what the fuck?"

"Don't you swear at me, and calm down. You're going to feel like an idiot in a minute."

He tilts his head.

"You remember agreeing it was okay for Shea to come for a visit?" I prod.

He nods. "Yeah."

"Well, she's here with her *husband. Carter.*"

Xander blinks. Looks at Shea and Carter, where they're standing arm-in-arm.

"Well, why didn't you say so? Carter fucking Winters! How the hell are ya? That was one hell of a season you had," Xander shouts, walking right up to Carter and hugging him.

I roll my eyes while the rest of the family laughs.

"Now *that* is the Xander I remember," Shea blurts out while she runs up and gives me a hug. "It's so good to see you."

"You, too. I've missed you."

And I have. So much. Shea and Carter came to visit at least twice a week. Then, when I was at a good point in therapy and I was able, we went out to dinner, too. They're still my best friends.

"Nice digs, Falling Down Rockstars." Shea whistles.

"Come here, brat," Linc calls out. She runs up and hugs him.

"How are you liking California?" she asks him.

He shrugs. "It's good. I'm content. Family's here."

Shea nods. "We may be moving this way soon. Carter doesn't want to re-up his contract with New York. Word is a couple teams out here want him."

"As well they should. MVP of the league," Xander boasts.

"You're an idiot," Carter tells Xan. "You've always been an idiot when it came to Tera. It's good to see none of that has changed."

Xander laughs. "Well, old habits die hard."

Carter playfully slaps Xander on the back. "Get over it, man. I never stood a chance, and we've all moved on."

"Jealousy isn't attractive," Lucy tells Xander.

Xander opens his mouth as if to say something and Lucy gives him a look. With that, he closes his mouth, points to her, and nods as if to say, "You're a fine one to be talking."

"You've got a baby bump!" Shea yells.

I laugh. "My belly seems to have exploded overnight."

"That's just how it happens," Lucy tells me.

Meggie and Trace come walking in and Meggie stands stock still.

"What is it?" Trace asks. He looks around then rolls his eyes and keeps walking.

"Is that..." Meggie begins, "Carter Winters?"

I nod.

"*The* Carter Winters?"

I nod again.

"I need to sit down. Then, I need to touch his biceps. Then, I need an autograph. In that order. Help me," she pleads, and Trace takes pity on her. He hoists her over his shoulder and leads her to the patio where everyone is headed.

We hang out all afternoon with the Winters'. It's so amazing that my two best friends got married. I knew they'd had random hookups in college, but I didn't know it ended up being so much more than that. I think they were afraid to tell me. I reassured them there was no need for that.

Tomorrow we fly to Chicago, but before that, I have something I need to do and I want to do it before it gets dark.

"Xander?"

"Yeah, babe."

"Can we go somewhere? Do we have to let someone know or can we just go? There's something I want to do," I tell him. Shea and Carter look at me just as funny as Xander does. They're all confused. But it'll become clear before long.

"I'll just let security know. They'll drive us. We always have at least two with us everywhere we go," Xan tells me.

I nod. "Okay. Good."

"Where are we going?" Shea asks.

I just look at her. Understanding dawns and she hugs me.

"Will Carter be okay?" I ask.

She nods. "I think so, but I'll give him a head's up, in case he'd rather not go."

"Okay."

"Um, is there something someone wants to tell us?" Meggie asks, holding up a positive pregnancy test.

Lucy gasps. "It's not mine!"

Jesse lets out a breath of relief. "Thank fuck for that."

"So, whose is it?" Trace asks.

Lucy looks around the room, eyeing Sera, Summer, and Meggie closely. "That's a really good question."

"It'd be best if whoever it is just confesses. That way Lucy will stop giving everyone those looks like you stole the last cookie from the cookie jar," Jesse informs us.

"Well, it's not mine. You already know I'm pregnant," I confess.

Trace looks at Meggie. "It's not yours, is it?"

She blanches. "No." Then she shudders.

"Visibly repulsed by the thought of having children. Good to know," Trace mutters.

I'm not sure if he's disappointed or relieved. It's hard to tell with those two.

"It's not mine," Nicole announces.

Lucy hugs her close. "You have your two children coming soon."

I think it's wonderful what they're doing for Luis and Maria. Adopting two wonderful children whose father was an abusive fuckface.

Sera laughs and hugs Cage. "It's not mine. Cage would be right there when I peed on a stick if I even thought I was PG."

Everyone looks at Summer, and Jace laughs. "Busted!"

Summer blushes. "I buried that beneath a bunch of Kleenex. Meggie, you're nasty."

"Don't even try to change the subject, woman," Meggie replies. "That's where you two took off to? Tsk tsk."

"You should really know better, Summer," Trace tells her. "Meggie has no boundaries."

"I know, but we were too excited to think about it. We didn't want to tell anyone yet. I'm only about eight weeks or so, I think," Summer tells us. "We'll know more when we go see Dr. Mac."

"Wow, my dad's got a lot of business coming his way," Xander declares as he walks back into the room. "Everything's ready if you are?"

I nod and look at Carter, who nods back.

"Where are you going?" Linc asks.

"To lay the past to rest," I answer.

Chapter Twenty-Nine

Tera

"ARE YOU OKAY?" Xander asks for the fifth time.

I nod, just looking out the window, taking in the sights. "I like to look out the window whenever I go somewhere now. I get to see everything I haven't for over a decade."

"Even if LA is mostly traffic?" he teases.

"Even if. It's soothing and calms my mind." I turn to look at him. "When we get back, I'll need to paint. I know we don't leave until late tonight, so that's okay, right?"

"Anything, Tera. You never have to ask," he assures me. He kisses my forehead. It's meant to be comforting, and it is. But as the SUV nears the gallery, I begin to shake.

"Tera," Carter calls softly.

I look at him. "I'm okay. This is something I talked through with my doctor. It's necessary, and she's on speed dial should I need her."

He looks skeptical, as does Shea.

I don't care. This isn't about them. It's about me. It's about what I need. I think Carter needs this, too, to see where... it happened.

The SUV stops, and I look at the front of the gallery, the large glass windows, the precious art beyond. It takes me a moment to muster the courage to open the door, but I do—well, I try to, but security beats me to it when I reach for the handle. They didn't touch it before. I'm sure Xander told them to give us time.

I step out of the SUV and notice a man in a suit standing on the side of the building.

Cage Nichols.

His hands are buried in his trouser pockets while he waits patiently, watching as I take the first step onto the concrete. I can't tell what he's thinking, I never can. His sunglasses shield his eyes, which makes it even more difficult.

I remove mine. I want to see everything clearly.

"Carter?" I call out.

"I'm here," he answers.

"You don't have to do this."

"Yes, I do."

"Okay." I take his hand in mine, then Xander's in the other.

"Cage," Xander says by way of greeting.

Cage just nods. "Security let me know you were coming here. I wanted to be here for you, Tera. I hope that's okay."

"It's more than okay. Thank you for your support," I answer. As Lucy said, he really is a gentle man to those he loves.

I let go of Xander and Carter's hands as we near the back of the building. My throat goes dry, my heart thumps so hard in my chest it almost hurts.

Fear. Anxiety. Post-traumatic stress.

Anger.

I walk to where my car was parked, as if on auto-pilot. The others follow at a distance. I don't even see them now. I'm back there, but not as me—as an observer.

"My car was parked right here. I was worried when I came out. It was after one in the morning. I was opening my car door when they called out. 'You dropped your scarf' is what he said. It wasn't mine. He knew that, though. It was a ploy to keep me from getting to safety. I realized my mistake too late, so I randomly dialed, hoping I'd reach someone. Anyone. I didn't know if I had or not. I just… hoped."

"They were talking. One mentioned art and how he does graffiti. I pretended my phone was dead when they wanted to put a phone number into it. I wanted to go. I told them I needed to go, but she leaned against the door. She was so pretty, but her eyes were hard, and it was in that moment, I knew I was in trouble."

"They told me it could go easy or they could do it the hard way. Even if I'd gone along with it, I knew they'd have hurt me as they did. He hated it when I didn't cry or scream."

I walk to the spot where they dragged me.

"I'm surprised some of my skin isn't still there."

"Jesus," Carter mutters.

"It was there," I point. "I don't know if it was minutes or hours, but it felt like an eternity in hell. I was grateful when I lost consciousness. I don't know what happened after that. I don't want to know. Ever."

I look to Carter. "How long do you suppose it was?"

He shakes his head. "I'm not sure. A long time, Tera. A long damn time."

I nod. My knees begin to shake when I see a spray paint can up against the side of an adjacent building.

You're safe. They're not here. It's in the past. You've overcome. You win.

I blink, and I snap back to reality. Cage stands next to me.

"I didn't know you then," he begins, "but you were married to Xander and he was family. That made you family."

I don't know what to say, where he's going, so I just remain quiet.

"I made sure those seven individuals would never hurt you again, Tera. The family protects its own," he tells me.

"What do you mean by that?"

"They've been removed from this world. They don't deserve to be here. Not after what they did to you. Not when I know they'd do it again, given the chance. They went to prison, and their sentence was delivered the first week behind bars."

"The sentence the 'family' gave them?" I ask.

He nods slightly, and only once. "The one I gave them." Now, he looks at me, removing his sunglasses. "No one will ever hurt you again, Tera."

The way he says it, so self-assured. There's no room for doubt.

I burst into tears. Tears of gratitude. Tears of relief. I throw my arms around Cage, and he holds me close while I purge the last of my grief—grief for all they took from me, grief for innocence lost.

I paint and paint and paint. I can't stop. The scene in my mind's eye is so vivid and vibrant. I only pause when Xander force feeds me a sandwich while I continue to paint, holding it up to my mouth for bites. He insists I drink milk, as well. Apparently, he and Dad have had a "conversation". I think that scares me a little.

"Wow," Shea breathes out when she enters the studio Xander set up for me. Two of the walls are nothing but windows. The ceiling has a large skylight. I fell in love the minute I saw it.

I keep painting while Shea reads a book in the chair in the corner. People come and go. I don't stop. Not until it's finished. I add my initials in the corner, TRM, and only then do I step back and assess my work. It's like nothing I've ever painted before. It's bright colors. It's happiness.

"That's incredible," Sera mutters behind me.

I wipe my hands on my paint cloth and set my brushes in the jar of cleaning solution.

I take a sip of the apple juice Xander left for me. I really need to pee. I've been holding it forever.

Lucy stands next to me. "You're so talented."

I don't say anything. I don't do well with compliments.

"You realize your paintings are scattered all throughout the house, right?" Lucy asks.

I nod. "I saw that. I see more and more as I explore this gigantic mansion. I asked Kennedy about them. He said to ask Jesse."

"Did you?"

"Not yet."

"I did," she confesses. "He told me he and the guys would make purchases here and there of your works and hang them everywhere to have a part of you here with them."

I nod and try hard not to cry. "They're the best brothers a girl could ask for. Even when they screw up."

Sera nods her agreement. "Are you going to sell this one?"

"No. This one's a gift."

"Lucky. I was going to ask to buy it," Sera adds.

"You'll get to see it anytime you want to. It's a gift for your husband," I tell her.

Her eyes widen, then go all dreamy.

"He helped me find my light. He committed grievous sins to make that possible. I'll never be able to thank him enough for that, so I want him to have the first look at that light," I explain.

"I'm honored," Cage says from the doorway.

I whirl around to look at him and smile.

"It needs to dry, and I'll have it framed, but this is for you. Thank you for all you've done for me, even when we'd never met," I praise.

He nods. "No thanks needed."

Lucy wraps an arm around me. "It's what family does."

Not all families, I think to myself. Not all families kill. Not all families sell weapons. Not all families commit crimes in the name of love and loyalty—but I bet they would if they could.

"I'm proud to be part of the family."

Chapter Thirty

Carter

"ARE YOU OKAY, love?" Shea asks when we get to our room.

I nod. "Yeah. No. I don't know. I needed to see it, where it happened. It brought closure, I think."

She hugs me. "I'm glad. If you need to talk, you know I'm here for you."

"I know. I'm a lucky guy."

"Don't you forget it," Shea teases.

"Never."

It's our usual repertoire, one I live for every day.

"I think this helped Tera a lot," Shea adds.

I nod. "Me too. And I'm glad they killed them."

"Agreed. It was such a heinous thing they did to our girl. I remember..."

I nod and swallow hard. "Me too."

"It's time to put that to rest, Carter. You were there for her. You *saved* her," Shea reminds me.

"Yeah. I used to battle the *what if I'd been able to get someone to her sooner*, but now, after all that shrink talk, I realize I did all I could do. I'm glad it was me she called," I admit.

"Me too."

"I could use a nap before we take off tonight. It'll be a long flight."

Shea yawns. "I'll join you. I'll set my phone alarm for an hour and a half. I still have to finish getting our things together."

"We'll do that together, baby. Let's go rest."

Chapter Thirty-One

Cage

I GET IN my car, lean back, and sigh. Within seconds, my phone rings, and without looking I know it's Giovanni.

"Nichols."

"How'd it go?" Gio asks.

"Very well. She found closure."

"Better than I could've hoped for. And the Winters boy?"

I chuckle. "Boy? Matches me at six-four and outweighs me by a good fifty pounds—and that's muscle. He's massive."

"He's still a boy to me. They're so young."

I grunt in agreement. "He seemed lost for a while. He looked lighter when he walked away. He's a hard read."

"For you, Nichols? That's a rare thing."

"I know. But they'll be okay. I told them. Tera cried and hugged me," I inform him.

"Good. I'm glad we could help. Are she and Xander solid?" he asks.

"As steel. Unbreakable."

"But…" he prods.

"She hasn't mentioned moving from New York." I tell him my concern.

"She will. Especially now that she faced her past. It'll all come in time, my boy," Gio assures me.

"We're off to Chicago tonight. I'll let you know when we land."

"Safe travels."

With that, the call ends.

Like Gio, I, too, am glad we could help them—all of them.

Chapter Thirty-Two

Xander

"How'd it go today?" Linc asks. We're on the plane, headed to Chicago, for the concert the day after to-morrow.

"Good. She got closure. Carter, too," I answer softly.

Linc nods. "Good."

"Why didn't you go?"

"I already went there, man, after one of my fights. After seeing the tapes..." His hands clench into fists. "I had to see for myself."

I nod. I'd been there before today, too. More times than I'll ever admit. The scene of the crime. The spot where those seven thugs changed the course of so many lives.

"They're dead," I blurt out.

He nods. "I figured. Family and all."

"Yeah," I breathe. I look down at Tera, who's fallen asleep against me, her head resting on my shoulder. I scooped her up and cradled her in my lap, Lucy covered her with a blanket, then I rested my hand on the baby bump.

I wonder how she's going to do at the concert. We've got a fifty-fifty chance. I hope it turns out for the better. If not, I'll finish out these charity shows, then retire from Falling Down. It's been a good run, but Tera has always meant more to me than the music. It took me almost losing her to realize that. I won't make that mistake twice.

Chapter Thirty-Three

Tera

YESTERDAY THE BANDS did their thing while I sketched anything and everything.

Xander whaling on the drums, grinning and singing along the entire time.

Jesse singing his heart out.

Ben fingering the strings of his guitar like it was an extension of his body.

Kennedy, eyes closed, feeling it all.

Ethan, head bobbing to the beat.

Then came Blush. They had the same passion in their expressions as the guys of Falling Down did.

I get it. I do. I *feel* it when they're up there. It's just such an important part of Xander. What if things don't work out? I've had massive anxiety all day and it's only the crew and workers. Plus, I've had four security guards around me the entire time.

I sigh at myself.

Will I be able to weather the storm ahead? We'll find out tomorrow.

The bands are already at the venue. When we pull up, people are *everywhere*. I start snapping my wristband. I take a deep breath, then nod to the security guard—Mike—that I'm ready.

I'm surrounded by men, each a foot taller and wider than me. You'd think I'd feel safe. Not quite. Maybe seventy-five percent.

It doesn't get any better when we enter the building. There are five bands playing today. Five played yesterday and five will play tomorrow, so there are people milling around everywhere.

I continue to snap my wristband.

Damian walks up. He is one tall, dark, and handsome son of a gun. And those startling green eyes. He is all kinds of hot.

"How're you doing, Tera?" is the first thing he asks.

"Anxious," I tell him honestly.

"I see that," he replies, looking to where I'm pulling the elastic strip constantly. "What can I do?"

"You're doing it. The rest is up to me, if I can handle things."

"Do you want to see Blush perform?" he asks.

I nod. "I'd love to."

We move forward to a spot off-stage that's been cleared for me.

I breathe out a breath of relief. "This is so much better. Thank you, Damian."

He nods. "I thought this would work best for you. There's a chair and headset if it gets too loud. I'm going to go check on the guys, but there's a team of six here for you if you need anything."

"Thank you," I shout over the music.

He winks and my heart flutters. Oh my, he's so pretty it's easy to forget he's also lethal.

I watch Lucy and crew perform. She owns that stage—they all do. It's not just a concert of watching a band stand there. Not for Blush. They take it to a whole other level. They sing and dance—speaking of dancing. Nicole's out there dancing like a pro with little Kadi. Kadi's got bright purple headphones on to protect her ears. They're all glittered and sparkled up. Adorable.

I can't help but smile. When Shea and Carter walk up, we start to dance—even Carter I-can't-dance Winters. The beat is too strong to resist.

All-too-soon they're coming off stage. They all hug and greet me—sweaty messes that they are. My mouth goes dry when Trace and Jace come off stage, shirtless, using said shirts to wipe the sweat from their faces.

"Oh my," Shea sighs. I nod in agreement. Carter's checking out Lucy's ass in her outfit.

I laugh. "We're all perving on our friends."

"Hell yeah, I am," Shea announces.

"Who better to perv on?" Carter asks.

"True enough. I need a water. I'll be right back," I tell them.

Shea touches my arm. "Someone can bring it to you if you want."

I shake my head. "I need to get used to it, right? Plus, I have security."

"Be careful," she tells me.

"Always."

We make it ten steps before I'm mobbed—but they can't get

to me. I'm surrounded by hulks. It's just—I get a bit claustrophobic not able to see beyond the walls of men. I duck between two of the guys and back into a corner.

"Are you okay?" Mike asks.

I nod. "I just needed space."

He nods in return. They stand close but not too close.

All these people. Wow.

"Falling Down's up next," Mike tells me.

I move forward and find the room with the beverages. I grab two bottles of water, putting one in my bag before heading back out. I bump into Kennedy.

"Steady there, little mama," he tells me, pulling me close for a hug. "You doing okay?"

I nod. "Fine. Crazy, right?"

"Awesome," he corrects.

"Baby," Xander yells with a huge smile. He's wearing a thin tank and basketball shorts. His signature band-ware.

"Hey," I return. "You look hot."

His eyes darken. "I can make time…" he teases.

"One of these times, I'm going to take you up on that. Show you how real women do quickies backstage," I taunt.

He holds his hands (drumsticks in those hands) over his chest. "Be still my heart, wife. You speak straight to my loins."

I laugh. "Did you seriously just say loins?"

He nods. "Loins, loins, loins. I'll set yours on fire later."

"Now you're talking."

"I'm gonna go out there with a semi," he announces.

I smirk. "You'll survive."

"Yes, I will, but later, I'll take that pent up sexual aggression out on you."

"Promises, promises."

"Them's fightin' words, woman," he retorts.

I wink.

He nods. "You wait 'til later," he says, pointing a drumstick at me.

"Will you let me play with your stick?" I ask, running a finger along the one pointed at me.

"Baby, you can play with anything you want. Damian, do we have ten, fifteen minutes?" he asks, and I shake my head.

"Go on now. Play with your friends. You can play with me tonight."

He points the drumstick again, then bites a fist, growling. He plants a kiss on my lips, dipping me back.

He growls again, setting me upright. And then he's gone.

"Holy hotness," Nicole declares.

I can only nod. Now, I'm worked up, too. My little game backfired.

We make our way back to side-stage and I watch my husband and brothers entertain tens of thousands of screaming fans. I couldn't be more proud.

When the show's almost over, Shea looks at me, smiling.

"What?" I ask.

"You haven't freaked out once."

My eyes widen in surprise when I realize she's right. I had more of an issue being surrounded by security than I did walking through a crowd in the hallway. I guess walking downtown helped. Being bumped and shoved by strangers must have toughened me up more than I thought.

I laugh; happy, giddy, knowing I can do this with Xander—knowing I *want* to be a part of this with him.

"You're going to do it, aren't you?"

I nod.

"We have to go," I tell her, pulling her hand.

"What? Where?"

"New York."

"Right *now?*" she screeches, and Carter laughs.

I nod. "*Now.*"

"At least wait for Xan—"

"Here they come," Carter cuts in.

Xander struts up after he throws his drumsticks out to the crowd. He's all sweaty and smiling and shirtless and happy. All of that—and he's mine.

"What's going on?" he asks.

I laugh, still a bit high on happiness.

"I can't do this anymore!" I shout at him.

"What?" he asks, his brows furrowing.

"I can't do this, I have to go."

"What? Where are you going?" he asks, beginning to panic, but I don't notice. I'm too amped up knowing I can finally do this, knowing I *am* going to do this.

"I need to go do this, Xan. I'll call you as soon as everything's settled. I promise." I hug him and kiss him hard on the lips. "I love you."

"I love you, too." He shakes his head, confused.

"I'll call, I promise!"

He nods, still confused.

I pull Shea, who pulls Carter, and we leave the arena.

"Know anyone we can borrow a plane from?" I ask.

"Let's just charter one," Carter tells me. "When we get on that flight, you need to explain to me what the hell just happened. Then you need to call your husband and explain it to him."

Chapter Thirty-Four

Xander

I STAND THERE, watching Tera, Shea, and Carter move through the crowd, wondering what the hell just happened.

Lucy looks at me in concern. "What's wrong?"

I shake my head. "I don't even know what the hell just happened. She said she couldn't do this anymore, laughing like it was the best thing in the world, then announced she had to go, told me she loved me, and promised to call me."

I stand there.

"What the fuck?"

Lucy can only blink. "Let me try calling her."

I nod. I don't have my phone. I don't have shit. I don't even have my wife. She just bailed.

"She wouldn't be happy like that if she didn't want to be with me, right?" I ask Lucy. "And she walked through the crowd without security and didn't panic." I pause. "*What the fuck!*"

Lucy grabs my hand. "Let's go find somewhere quiet so we can find out what the fuck."

I nod and follow blindly behind her.

I'm so confused.

If she leaves me again, I won't survive it.

Chapter Thirty-Five

Lucy

I THINK I know what's going on, but I need to find out for sure. I've been trying to reach Tera for three days.

"Fuck this," Xan spits out. "I'm going to find her."

"You don't even know *where* she is," I reason.

"I'll find her," he insists.

"Sit down, brother," Linc urges. He hands Xan a beer. "Relax. We'll figure it out."

I walk out of the room and dial Tera for the thousandth time, losing my patience.

"Hello?" Tera answers.

"Finally!" I shout. "Where the hell did you go?"

"Um," Tera replies. "I'm in New York."

"Is there a reason why you haven't been answering your phone?"

"I left it on the plane we chartered. Today was the first day I had time to go get a new one," she explains.

"You didn't have time over the last three days?" I bite out, a bit pissed.

"No. I was busy packing."

I pause. Packing could be good.

"Explain to me, please, what the hell is happening right now," I plead.

She explains. I listen. Then she asks me for a favor.

I really, really like her.

Thirty-Six

Tera

"How did you manage to come here and him not come with?" I ask Lucy and Sera.

Lucy blows out a breath and rolls her eyes. "It was *not* easy. He kept on insisting."

"He's going nuts not being able to talk to you. Good deal calling while he was in the shower and leaving voicemails," Sera tells me. "Well done."

"I didn't want him to be that upset, not to the point he was. I mean, him talking about quitting the band—yikes," I say.

"Yeah, he was tormented those first three days. You coulda planned that a little better for the sake of my sanity," Lucy tells me.

I wince. "Sorry. I just wanted to pack everything, so it could be shipped while everyone was here, in New York, for the concert."

"I got the permission we needed. How exactly do you want to do this?" Lucy asks me.

"Here's what I had in mind…"

I feel like I'm going to puke and it has nothing to do with the baby in my ever-expanding belly. There's no doubt now that I'm pregnant. I had to get stretchy jeans. I hate them. I'll stick to my yoga pants and leggings.

"Hurry up!" Lucy whisper shouts, pushing me into a room backstage. She yells, "Zip it!" to Spenser, just as he's about to do that squeal/yell thing he does when he's excited.

"I knew it! I knew it, I knew it, I *knew* it!" he exclaims, rushing toward me to hug me. "Oh my, how our little bambino has grown in a week."

I sigh. "I know. This is going to be massive."

Lucy nods. "And then some. Jesse's been wondering what's going on since they're going on before we are, but I've been keeping this secret."

"Thank you. I know it can't be easy," I tell her.

"Whatever," she waves it off, "he kept you a secret for the entire time we've been together, he can deal."

I laugh.

"Let's get you fixed up," Spenser announces, pulling me away from Sera and Lucy. Meggie bounces in, Trace and Jace following close behind.

"I can't even tell you how excited I am," Meggie laughs out as she continues to bounce on the balls of her feet.

"We can see," Trace tells her. "I gotta tell you, Tera. You sure know how to make a statement."

I blow out a breath as Spenser works his magic.

"Let's just hope it works."

Damian sneaks me around to the other side of the stage. It's cluttered with containers and boxes for all the bands' gear.

He catches me when I nearly trip over a cord.

"That's why no one goes on this side of the stage," he informs me.

"I see."

"Be careful. They're almost done, and you don't want to be seen, right?"

I nod. "I'll stand here. You can keep an eye out."

The wait for Falling Down to clear the stage and the crew to set up Blush's equipment seems to take forever. I knew it would be a good forty-five minutes to an hour. I should have brought something to occupy my hands. I wouldn't have been able to focus, anyway. Not when my heart is threatening to leap up through my throat. My stomach is still flip-flopping, and I'll admit to my knees being a bit weak.

I peek out and see all the people. I gulp. "That's a lot of people."

"What did you expect for Madison Square Garden?" he asks. "Remember, you won't be able to see too much when the lighting is on you, so pretend it's only Lucy and Sera there, just like you practiced."

"Good idea. I hope it works."

"You're saying that a lot. Have faith. This is going to be epic.

The press and the fans are going to eat this up," he assures me.

"That's not helping to calm me down. What if I throw up out there?" I wonder aloud.

"You won't be the first nor the last."

"Great," I reply wryly. Some help he is.

"Here we go," Damian tells me. They announce Blush and the music starts. They play their first song then yell to the crowd.

"Oh God, oh God, oh God."

"Go get 'em, Tera," Damian tells me with a smack on the ass. I'm wearing casual attire. Leggings, biker boots, a black and pink Blush tank. Spenser left my hair down, stating it'd be better for the photos.

I walk out on shaky legs.

"We have a surprise for you all! A very special guest is joining us on stage tonight!" Lucy shouts.

I make my way out there, fiddling with the ear piece. Like I'm going to be able to work this thing.

The crowd cheers, but I can tell there's confusion.

"You're probably wondering who this is, am I right?" Meggie asks.

The crowd shouts a resounding "yes".

"Well, my friends, this is our friend, part of our family, and famous painter Tera Ramirez Mackenzie!" Sera shouts. "She dropped the 'Ramirez' when she and Xander said their 'I do's' over a decade ago!"

The crowd goes wild.

I wave and take a seat on the stool they put out for me. Lucy and Sera take seats on the stools on either side of me.

"Hi everyone!" I shout. "I'm a little nervous. It's my first time on stage."

"We popped her cherry, Madison Square Garden!" Jace shouts.

The cheers are deafening. *Now* I understand the ear piece.

"I have a story to tell you and then we'd like to sing you a little song. How does that sound?" I ask.

I tell them mine and Xander's story, how we met up until now, leaving out all the details. Glossing over the reasons we were apart by calling them "misunderstandings". Then I explain why I wanted to be kept out of the spotlight.

"But now I'm ready to stand in the light right next to the man I love. My husband, Xander Mackenzie!" I shout.

Now's about the time he's supposed to be walking out here... but he's not.

Damian talks in my ear. "He doesn't want to go back out. Jesse's dragging him down the hall now. Just go on and sing. He'll hear it."

"Looks like the Xan Man has a little stage fright," Lucy mocks. "We don't need him anyway. Sing for 'em, Tera."

They play the music and I sing. We use the melody to the song Xander wrote when we were apart: Forever Blue. I changed the lyrics to make it fit our situation, to make it happier.

Come out here, walk on stage, I want you to know
I've been looking for you, come join the show
You're a diamond in the rough, a true gem to find
You're my soulmate, always on my mind

I'm here now, here to be with you
I walked in the door and since then it's been forever you
A girl in pigtails, I didn't have a clue
You stole my heart and every day since it's been forever you.

Together and apart, we found a way to
Find our way back to one another, always and forever you
My husband, your wife, we make each other whole
A love I feel down to my soul

No one will love you better than me, Xan
No love purer than that of my husband

I will never leave you alone, this I promise you
Since you walked in the door it's been forever you
I love the way you do what you do
You own my heart, it'll always be forever you.

The crowd has their cell phones and lighters raised when I open my eyes. I feel him behind me. I felt him when I began to sing, but I knew if I looked at him, I'd never make it through the song.

"Tera Mackenzie, serenading her husband, everybody!" Lucy cheers.

I turn to him now, his cheeks wet with tears.

"You sound a hell of a lot better than you did that day on the playground," he tells me and everyone laughs.

"Thank God."

"I was so afraid you'd left."

I shake my head. "Never. Never again. I knew I wanted this, all of this, with you."

He pulls me to him and hugs me so tight. I hug him, too.

"I packed my apartment. Everything should be there when we get home," I tell him, Lucy holding the mic close so everyone can hear. Oh boy.

"Jesus, I thought you left. I was ready to quit, to give everything up and come to you," he confesses, his body shaking.

"Why would you want to do that when I don't have to give up anything to be in LA with you? I gain a family. It's win-win," I murmur.

"I love you so fucking much, Tera."

"I love you so fucking much, too, Xan."

The audience laughs.

"You said home. You're finally coming home," he whispers.

"Xander," I pull back. "I'm already home."

He hugs me tight again.

"Did she tell you?" he asks. "We're having a baby!"

Cheers explode, making it hard to hear myself think. On second thought, I've done enough thinking. It's time to live, instead.

Epilogue

Xander

"**P**USH, TERA. JUST a little more," Dad tells Tera.

"Screw you. You push. Just a little more. I'll give you a little more," she yells.

"Good, let's go!" he replies. He's got bigger balls than I do. I'd never in a million years say that to Tera right now.

She growls and digs deep, pushing hard. I'm sitting behind her, helping to support her back while she leans forward, giving it all she's got to give birth to our baby.

I think I've said two words. I'm scared shitless. She's in so much pain and Dad's acting like this is normal. This cannot be normal. I feel how hard her stomach tightens.

"There's the head," Dad praises and Tera pants.

I lean over her shoulder to take a look. I make a face at all the goo and blood and Tera snickers. "You should see your face right now."

I grin. "All that… goo and blood." I scrunch up my nose.

"I'm totally not looking. I don't want to see how big my vagina has gotten to accommodate this child," she pants.

"It all goes back to normal," Dad reminds her. "Do Kegels."

"Kegel this," she says, giving him the finger.

Dad laughs. "I know you don't really mean that. It's the pain talking."

"No, it's really not. I mean it. I mean it a whole fuck of a lot," she replies.

Dad just laughs more.

"Dad," I begin, "ixnay on the aughinglay."

He laughs again.

"You got a death wish, old man?" I ask, in shock.

"One more little push, not too hard, Tera. You're a superstar," he croons.

"Damn right I'm a superstar," she answers. "Just look at this baby hanging out of my vajayjay." A contraction hits and she groans, pushing a bit, and out slips the baby.

"Whoa," I mutter.

"It's a baby girl!" Dad announces. "Do you wanna cut the cord?"

"I don't want to move," I tell him.

"No worries."

They bring the baby close and hand me some scissor-like thingies to cut the cord. It's kinda gross, really. I get mesmerized by our daughter as the nurse suctions her mouth and nose, and a second nurse cleans off the gunk. Yuck.

"Jesus, Tera. Look at her. She's so small. Look, her face is all scrunched up just like yours does when I fart. And look at all that dark hair," I ramble.

"It's no wonder you had heartburn," I continue. I read that in a book somewhere. I think Tera thinks it's bullshit, but I think it's all true.

"Hold the phone!" Dad yells.

I sit up, and so does Tera.

"What's going on?" I ask.

"Is that a foot?" Sandy asks, and my skin grows cold. I begin to sweat.

"What?" I squeak.

"Damn, would you look at that," Dad announces.

"What are we looking at!" I yell. "Answer me, old man!"

He looks up at me, the baby crying in the background while the nurse swaddles her, his eyes crinkled in laughter.

"Just kidding!" he tells me with a laugh.

"You are in so much trouble, old man," I begin, then notice Tera's shoulders shaking with laughter. "You!" I accuse. "You were in on this?!"

She laughs even harder, then groans when Dad does something down there.

"I think I peed my pants a little," I confess.

"Life with you is never going to be boring," Tera tells me through her giggles.

"You know it. I'm full of all kinds of fun, and everyone knows life is more fun with a little Xananigans."

THE END

Like the book? Please consider leaving a review.

Join the Facebook group for exclusive content
http://bit.ly/AMfamiglia

Stay up to date on all things Anne Mercier
http://eepurl.com/buLAUb

For free stuff, giveaways, and ARC entries,
please fill out these forms.
US Residents: https://goo.gl/BJbEJQ
International: https://goo.gl/DPZ9

Acknowledgments

Wow, I have so many people to thank.

Thank you, Shelly, for being so supportive.

Thank you, Mom, for always encouraging me to keep writing.

Tons of thanks to all of you, the readers, for sticking with me through the rough times.

To the members of the Facebook La Famiglia group—I adore you. Every day you make me smile. I feel like the luckiest person/author ever. I have the best readers and friends EVER!

Super thanks to the bloggers. You are marvelous! You are invaluable. You promote me and my books so selflessly—words will never be enough to thank you.

To the Sparkly Ladies, my beta group: Your feedback and help is priceless. Thank you for being available at odd hours to give me your thoughts and opinions as well as making sure no plot hole goes unfilled! Mwah!

To Mandi Wathey—My sister from another mister: I adore you. Thank you so much for unwavering support and love.

To Nicole Bailey—You're more than my editor. You're my friend. My title brainstormer. My go-to person when I'm feeling unsure. You're honest and forthright and I couldn't appreciate that more!

I can't imagine my life without you! I can't imagine writing a book without you!

To Melissa Mendoza—my amazing personal assistant and friend. For all you do, words will never be enough. I value you and everything you do for me and with me. I value our working relationship and our friendship. I love that we can have both. I can't wait to meet you in September! Be prepared for long hugs and likely tears.

I'm positive I'm forgetting people and for that I'm sorry.

XANDER: PART 2, THE PRESENT

Playlist

AVAILABLE ON SPOTIFY AND YOUTUBE

Try—Colbie Caillat

Broken—Seether, Amy Lee

Cry Pretty—Carrie Underwood

Say Something—A Great Big World

Wherever You Will Go—The Calling

Stay With me—Sam Smith

Little Too Late—Default

Sad Song (Feat. Elena Coats)—We The Kings

I Can't Fall In Love Without you—Zara Larsson

California King Bed—Rihanna

100 In A 55—Pop Evil

Alone In This Bed (Capeside)—Framing Hanley

Million Reasons—Lady Gaga

Forever and Always—Parachute

Lips of an Angel—Hinder

Landing In London—3 Doors Down

Far Away—Nickelback

Stay—SafetySuit

All Or Nothing—Theory of a Deadman

Here's To The Heartache—Nothing More

Just Between You And Me—Lou Gramm

Here Without You—3 Doors Down

If Only For Now—Pop Evil

By The Way—Theory of a Deadman

Wild Is The Wind—Bon Jovi

Clarity—Zedd, Foxes

I'm Not The Only One—Sam Smith

Dreaming With A Broken Heart—John Mayer

Still—Commodores

Where I Stood—Missy Higgins

Rain—Breaking Benjamin

Purpose—Justin Bieber

Second Chance—Shinedown

Born To Be My Baby—Bon Jovi

I Can't Not Love You—Every Avenue

Talking Body—Tove Lo

Tell Her You Love Her—Echosmith

There You Are—Jaymes Reunion

Amanda's Song (C.M. Version)—Jason Koiter

Say You Won't Let Go—James Arthur

Perfect—Ed Sheeran

You and Me—Lifehouse

Photograph—Ed Sheeran

Home—Daughtry

A Thousand Years—Christina Perri

Collide—Howie Day

Bubbly—Colbie Caillat

Your Body Is A Wonderland—John Mayer

Sunday Morning—Maroon 5

Little Things—One Direction

Lay Me Down—Sam Smith & John Legend

Beneath Your Beautiful—Labrinth, Emeli Sandé'

You & I—One Direction

They Don't Know About Us—One Direction

How Long Will I Love You—Ellie Goulding

Uncover—Zara Larsson

Million Reasons—Lady Gaga

Love Me Like You Do—Ellie Goulding

Say—John Mayer

She Is Love—Parachute

Just A Kiss—Lady Antebellum

Love Song—Sara Bareilles

Everything—Michael Bublé'

Gravity—Sara Bareilles

Hanging By A Moment—Lifehouse

Bright—Echosmith

Smile—Uncle Kracker

Kiss Me—Sixpence None The Richer

Put Your Records On—Corrine Bailey Rae

Not A Bad Thing—Justin Timberlake

You Give Me Something—James Morrison

Come Away With Me—Norah Jones

I Do (Cherish You)—98 Degrees

I Knew I Loved You—Savage Garden

Perfect Color (Acoustic Version)—Safetysuit

This Goes Out To You—Adelitas Way

I Was Made For Loving You—Tori Kelly, Ed Sheeran

Burning—Sam Smith

First Time—Kygo, Ellie Goulding

With Love—Christina Grimmie

Kiss Me Slowly—Parachute

Love Remains The Same—Gavin Rossdale

Gravity—John Mayer

She's My Kind Of Rain—Tim McGraw

Raining On Sunday—Keith Urban

Back To Us—Rascal Flatts

I Run To You—Lady Antebellum

Somebody Like You—Keith Urban

Do You—Spoon

Kissing Strangers—DNCE, Nicki Minaj

Island In The Sun—Weezer

Never There—Cake

Every Morning—Sugar Ray

Pretty Fly (For A White Guy)—The Offspring

Pulse:
#JUCY and #SAGE short story
Rockstar #15

ROCKSTAR

Bestsellling Author
Anne Mercier

Pulse
Rockstar Book 15
Copyright ©2018 Anne Mercier
ISBN: 9780996262170
All rights reserved.

This is a work of fiction. Names, characters, businesses, places, events, and incidents are products of the author's imagination and are used fictitiously. Any resemblance to actual persons, living or dead, events or locales is purely coincidental.

Cover Image: Sara Eirew at Sara Eirew Photography.
Cover Design: Anne Mercier.

PERSONAL NOTE: The only pirate I like is Johnny Depp as Captain Jack Sparrow, which means I'd appreciate if you'd keep my books to yourself. Pirating shows a clear lack of respect for the author—me. I'd rather not meet you on bad terms, so let's not do that, let's not meet that way. Let's meet at a signing or conference instead, or let's go have a cup of coffee or a drink. Thank you for respecting the time and effort put into each book. I appreciate it very much.

PULSE
Rockstar Book 15
a #JUCY and #SAGE short story

Jesse and Lucy need a break. They look and feel like cast members from The Walking Dead, and I'm not talking about the humans. It's only an overnight break, but it's exactly what they need.

Cage and Sera attend a charity function and run into an unwelcome enemy. They spend a special night together before they get to work on a plan of how to keep one of their own safe.

Dedication

Melissa—the best friend and PA a girl could ever have.
Thank you for your support, your friendship, your kindness,
listening when I need to talk something out, and for offering
advice when I need it. I appreciate you more than words can say…
this one's for you.

Chapter One

Sera

CHARITY FUNCTIONS ARE fun when they're like this one. It's not formal and it's bidding and it's all about taking care of animals—endangered species to be exact. The room is filled with the wealthy socialites I've come to know and definitely not respect. They think money can buy reverence; I prefer actions. So far, I'm not impressed.

We're standing, thumbing through the pamphlet looking at all the creatures who are entirely too beautiful to let fade away. Some are well known, others are not.

African wild dog.
Amur leopard.

Amur tiger.

Asian elephant.

Bengal tiger.

Black-footed ferret.

When we get to the black rhino, Cage rubs his thumb over the image.

"What is it?"

His mouth is set in a hard line. "I know someone who hunts these."

"Let's hunt him. See how he likes it." My blood is boiling. Hunting defenseless animals like that. Arrogant, entitled prick.

Cage's lips twitch. "My darling Fee, I'd love nothing more."

"Let's do it. A game of cat and mouse."

"Hmm," is all he says, but I know that means he's thinking about it. Fun, fun, fun for me!

Now I laugh out loud and Cage raises his brows. I point to the image. Black spider monkey. "Lucy."

His lips twitch again.

I page through the pamphlet and I'm heart broken. I just can't...

"Fee."

I look at my gorgeous husband and pout. "I can't pick just one. Can we support more than one?"

"We can support them all if you like. We can spread our donation out. We can also pursue other avenues to help these animals," he informs me.

I lean in and hug him. "Thank you."

"Fee, you never have to thank me. I'd do anything for you."

And just like that, I'm a complete puddle of goo again. This man. This quietly controlled, formidable man can bring the best of opponents down to his knees. I won't even mention what he does to the worst. But me, he cherishes. He treats me like a queen and loves me so completely, I'll never get enough. Ever.

I'm pondering how I got so lucky, when I feel it. I don't make it obvious. I just slide my eyes, looking around the room. It's then that I see him. Dark hair. Large build. Mean mug.

I continue looking about the room, and still he stares.

"I don't know who that is, but he keeps staring at me," I whisper to Cage.

"Fee. You're so beautiful everyone can't help but stare," he replies.

I melt a little inside at his words. No matter how many times he tells me I'm beautiful or how much he loves me, it feels like the first time.

I slide my eyes in the same direction of tall, dark, and creepy, and he's still staring. Blatantly.

"Babe," I nudge him with my elbow.

"I see him. Just… act like you don't. Damian's on it."

I want to look behind us to see exactly what Damian's doing, but I don't. I know better. I've been trained better. I, just once, would like to see the Enforcers do their thing where I'm not the thing they're doing.

Wait.

That sounded so dirty. I bite back a smile, calling on my discipline to show nothing but indifference. I've gotten so well at it, my family's starting to worry. Well, the ones who aren't involved in la Famiglia.

"Is he familiar?" I purr into Cage's ear as I curl into his side, pressing my breasts against his arm, playing the role. It's amusing to me when people assume I'm arm candy and nothing more. They sure do get a rude awakening when I pull out my gun or knife, or just kick their ass in hand-to-hand. The best is the men—the big, muscular ones who think that's enough to get by.

Not in this business. In this business you need to be lethal, constantly alert, and not afraid to get hurt or even to die. Not many women are that dedicated which is why there are only a small handful. Me, Celeste, Bella—we set the tone. Really, Celeste set the tone. She was in the business as long as Cage, though not always in a physical sense. She started out doing leg work, paperwork, all the mundane shit they give women to do. She was also a very young sixteen when she and Cage became friends in Joan's group home, Harmony House. Damian was a part of that group, too. I'm sure there are others that I haven't learned about yet, but this is the inner circle of it all.

Cage's body tenses up and I look up to see what's wrong.

"I know who he is. We need to leave. Now," is all he says before he wraps an arm around me and we leisurely weave our way through the crowded room.

I feel his gaze on us as we exit the building, and I know what Cage is about to tell me isn't going to be good.

Chapter Two

Lucy

THE CHAOS SURROUNDING me as Jesse and I get ready to walk out the door makes me want to rip my hair out. Four toddlers, three children, and umpteen adults all talking at the same time. So, I do what any good mother does. I soothe my children.

"We'll only be gone overnight. Uncle Xan, Aunt Tera, Aunt Summer, Uncle Ethan, Aunt Nicole, and Uncle Ben will be taking care of you. You can play with Kadi and Maria and Antonio. Daddy and I will be back at lunchtime, okay? The boys nod, Kiki cocks her head to the side. "Okay mama."

I hug them all and tell them I love them as does Jesse then, finally, we're out the door—thirty minutes later than planned. We climb into the back of the car—security. Always security. Never a moment to ourselves anymore. We need this overnight—I need this overnight. I'm feeling claustrophobic in my life. I feel guilty for it. I love my family. I truly do. I just need a breather. Just—peace. Just—Jesse.

"Almost there, Cupcake," Jesse informs me. I've been staring blankly out of the window, not seeing the sunshine, not seeing the people, not seeing the beauty of life.

"I'm sorry, Jesse."

"Don't be. Never be sorry for how you feel. Truth is, I could use some down time myself," he admits.

I look at him hopeful. "Really?"

He nods.

I let out a relieved breath. "I've been feeling like such a horrible mother and friend. I swear to you, one more night in that house would likely drive me insane. I was ready to make a break for it."

Jesse intertwines his fingers with mine. "Not without me, you don't."

"No," I realize. "I could never go without you." I rest my head on his shoulder.

"Luce. We've gone damn near three years without a break from everyone and everything. We went from meeting, recording, tour-ing, having kids, writing, recording, touring, and now we're back to writing songs. It's okay to need a recharge. Hell, I could sleep for 48 hours straight without blinking an eye."

I snicker. "The apple of your eye, your she-devil, only wants her daddy now. Well, you and Princess RaRa."

"Tera does kinda look like that Princess Jasmine a little."

I nod against him. "I see it. Never a dull moment with Kiki, that's for sure."

"Lord have mercy. I'm so grateful we didn't have four girls. I'd be institutionalized."

At that I laugh. I can't help it. "Kiki is definitely a handful. She's not a brat. She's not a pain in the ass. She's just... spirited."

"I beg to differ, baby. She definitely can be a pain in the ass. Especially when she interrupts some amazing sex that I know is going to end in a phenomenal orgasm," Jesse disputes.

"Oh, God. You're so right on that part. That one night..."

His hand gently squeezes mine when I let out a moan.

"Don't even remind me. You were right there and I'd been hanging on the edge, trying to make it last just a little longer. God damn, it felt so good. To turn up the heat a bit between us and hear Kiki ask us what we're doing—"

"—From right next to the bed."

Jesse groans. "I wanted to send her out for just one more minute so we could both come. Worst case of blue balls in the history of blue balls."

"Is there a female version of blue balls?" I wonder aloud.

Jesse chuckles. "I don't know but if there is, you fucking had it that night."

I tilt my head up to look at him from where my head's still resting on his shoulder. "How does she always know?"

He rubs his free hand over his face then lets out a chuckle. "Fuck if I know, but that kid has radar for anyone fucking. Did Xander tell you about the time he and Tera were fucking in the shower and Kiki kept pounding on the door?"

This time I let out a loud laugh. "Serves him right for spoiling her like he did. And now with her obsession with Princess RaRa..." I laugh again. Kiki stopped in her tracks the first time she saw Tera. She just stopped and stared. Her face full of wonder and surprise. She told Tera she looked like Princess Jasmine from Aladdin and ever since then, they've been best princess pals. I am in no way jealous of their bond. I'm grateful she can brush someone else's hair and tell all her tales. She needs more than just me--as much as I'd love to keep her all to myself.

The car stops.

"We're here," Jesse mutters. "Thank Christ, we're here."

I moan longingly for the silence and the comfort of a bed no children will be crawling into, doors no one will be knocking on unless we request it. We're on the top floor—extravagant for one night, but fuh-huhu-uck me I'm exhausted.

Chapter Three

Cage

WE GET TO the car and I immediately dial Gio. He picks up on the second ring.

"Tell me," he says as if he already knows it's a shitstorm in the making.

"Murphy."

I hear him shift in his chair swearing under his breath.

"Was it him or one of his men?" Gio asks.

"One of his top guys. Kept staring at Serafina," I tell him through gritted teeth. I didn't let on just how much that pissed me off. Everyone looks at her. She's a beauty like no other. But him. He stared even when he was caught. A blatant show of disrespect.

"We'll meet at eight tomorrow. This needs to be contained." He pauses. "Have you told her yet?"

"No, but I will."

"She's going to want to intervene."

I can't hide the pride in my voice even with the annoyance that thought brings me. "Of course she will. She's one of us."

He lets out a sigh. "So she is. You talk with her. I'll call Frank."

"Done."

With that, we hang up. She's watching me, my Fee. The woman who loves me so much I can feel it. The woman I love so much it hurts. The woman I'd die for. My wife. My life. My forever.

"Straight up?" I ask her.

She nods. "Always."

"Murphy is Nicole's father."

She immediately sits ramrod straight, her face flush with emotion. "No."

"That was one of his crew we saw tonight and he showed a very clear disrespect for who we are and who we represent."

"They know?"

I nod.

"Are they…?"

"No. He'd like to think so. He isn't held in high enough esteem. He's a mean bastard and the turnover of his crew is a lot."

"I notice you say 'crew' whereas we're Famiglia?" Fee questions.

I nod. "Few stay with him long enough for him to have a large enough group and he's killed all but one of his brothers."

"Jesus, Cage. What are we going to do? She just got well. She's doing so great in school. And those babies…" my Fee frets and worries. She's taken a special liking to Coley. She admires her strength. I think in some ways she sees a bit of herself in the young lady.

"We're meeting at the house at eight tomorrow. Gio knows you'll want to be involved. He's calling Frank," I reiterate.

"Oh my God. I didn't even think of Frank." She sits back and slumps into the seat, looking out the window as the lights glow in the darkness of night.

I pull her over into my lap and hold her close.

"It'll be okay, Fee. We'll handle him. He's nothing compared to la Famiglia."

"He wants to hurt her. I know he does. He wants to hurt her for leaving and evading him for God knows how many years. He'll hurt her then he'll kill her," she says softly.

"We won't let that happen. I'll snap his neck before he gets close, though he'd have to get past Damian first. He cares deeply for her," I divulge.

"No way," she exclaims, looking up at me.

I chuckle. "Not like that. Like she and Kennedy are. They connected on a different level than she did with anyone else. Likely because he was on the run for a long time, too."

"I didn't know that. I don't know much about Damian's past and he doesn't talk about it."

"Of course, you've asked," I tease.

"Well, yeah. It's Damian. He's important to me," she admits.

I nod. "One day he'll tell you his story. I would, but it's not mine to tell. I will tell you he was one of Joan's kids the same time I was. It's how we met. Celeste too."

"Celeste too? Wow. She's a little younger than you, isn't she?"

"Yes. Six years. Damian's younger by three years. We were quite the mix," I confess with a wry grin. "Those were hard times for all of us."

"I know, baby," Fee coos, then hugs me tightly to her.

"I never thought I'd make it to thirty-two. I certainly never even imagined I'd be married to the woman I've loved for nearly half my life."

"But here you are. Cage Nichols. Successful business man. Friend to many. In some ways you care for others the way Lucy does, it's just not as obvious. Wonderful husband. Phenomenal lover. My very best friend. You made this of yourself, baby. You. No one else. I am so proud of you and all you've become," my Fee whispers to me sweetly.

"I love you so much I don't know how to contain it sometimes. I want to hug you so tightly you're never away from me. I want to tuck you away in my pocket for safe keeping."

She snorts. "You only want me in your pants so I'm closer to your cock."

I lift a brow. "That would be an added bonus."

"Mhmm," she purrs. She curls into me a little more. She must have forgot her wrap again and it's unusually cool for February in California.

I open my jacket and wrap her up in it with me. I'd take it off, but I'm too greedy to let her go. It's not often I get private moments like these with my wife. At home, yes; but everywhere else, no. We usually have someone with us, not just a driver. I didn't want to wait, and Damian had things to do. If I saw one of Murphy's men there, I know there were more. I trust my Enforcer and best friend to get all the information he can—and he will. Damian Black is a man not to be fucked with.

Chapter Four

Jesse

WE GET TO the room and Lucy heads to the bedroom. "We do not want to be disturbed under any circumstances. Well, unless the building is on fire, but really, we're on the top floor so it wouldn't really matter, would it?" I pause. I fucking sound like Xander right now. God, I'm tired.

"Yes, Sir. We have your 'Do Not Disturb' order unless otherwise requested. Would you like the bags in the bedroom?" This poor bellhop or whatever the hell they call them, putting up with the demands. He's a good kid, though. He's not even making a big deal about who I am or who Lucy is.

"Here's just fine. Hey, man, thanks for handling all our shit." I slip him a C-note. Just the softness of his voice earned half that.

"Wow, thank you, Sir. If you need anything, please don't hesitate to call down."

With that, he leaves the room and I lock the door. I head to the bedroom where Lucy's lying flat on her back, feet dangling off the end of the bed.

"You collapsed into the cushiony goodness without me," I berate.

"Jesse," she whispers.

"Huh?" I grunt as I collapse next to her.

"Do you hear that?"

I pause. "What?"

"Nothing. Oh, dear God in Heaven, nothing!"

"I'd laugh but I'm too tired. Would you be disappointed if we took a nap before I fuck you 'till you scream?"

"Not even one little bit. Don't think of waking me either. I'm sleeping until I can't anymore," she warns me with a finger point.

I whistle. "That finger point is serious business."

"You bet it is."

"You're so cute when you're feisty," I admire.

"I'm too tired to be feisty. I'm too tired to worry about anything so I'm just getting naked and crawling into this big, wonderful, soft, cushiony bed and sleeping. I'm not even sorry about the snoring about to happen."

I do chuckle at that. "I'm not sorry either."

"I think a freight train could come through here and I wouldn't wake up. I know there are no kids here to listen for. I haven't had a solid night's sleep since the babies were born. That's almost three years, Jesse. No wonder I'm so pale and have circles under my eyes. Having kids has made me old and ugly," she complains.

"Nah. You're as gorgeous as you ever were. You see these dark circles?" I point to my eyes. "You saw the gray hair I pulled out yesterday. A gray hair. Luce, I'm barely thirty and I'm getting gray hair."

"Darling, you're as hot and sexy as ever," Lucy murmurs as she slides under the covers. She hands me a sleep mask. It's pink.

"What the fuck? It's pink."

"Who fucking cares, Jesse. Get naked, put it on, and let's get some sleep. Your gray hair and manliness can be discussed later. Oh my, this feels so good," she lets out a moan.

"Damn it. I'm jealous. You're already in there." I strip as quickly as I can to my boxer briefs and climb in beside her. "This is what I'm talking about." I slip the sleep mask on to block out the light. "No pictures with this thing on." I give her a look.

She smirks with her eyes closed. "No way. No Xananigans here."

"Thank fuck."

That's the last thing either of us says. We both crash out within minutes.

Chapter Five

Xander

"DUDE, DID YOU see them? They looked like fucking zombies when they walked out the door."

Ethan nods. "It was getting pretty bad. They should've taken the whole weekend."

"They wouldn't. Not their first time away," Summer adds.

"That's true," Xan agrees. "I'm just glad this is something we could give them to help them get back to feeling human again. They should do this every other month. No lie. I don't know how they do it, running on no sleep."

"You'll find out soon enough," Linc reminds me with a hand clasp on my shoulder.

"Oh God," Tera groans.

"We're only having one. We're good, babe," I reassure her.

Kennedy snickers. "Dude. Jesse and Lucy never expected to hear they were having three, and then they found a bonus baby on top of it. Never say never."

I drop to my knees, look up, and fold my hands in prayer.

"Please Lord. Only one baby at a time. Happy healthy babies, but only one—two if you have to, but please. No more than that," I pray. Well, it's more begging than praying.

"You better hope he heard you," Linc advises.

I hang my head. I don't know if I'd survive more than one or two at a time. But if that's what comes our way, I'll take it. I'll love those kids so much they'll never doubt it.

It was easy "playing" dad when I snuck one of the babies for the night—or day. But I know it's a hell of a lot different when they're your own. You can't give them back. You can't only parent them for one hour or even one day. It's a 24/7 job and one I think Tera and I can handle it. Look how well we handled things while we were apart—except for that one time…

I know, together we can handle anything.

Chapter Six

Damian

"I MADE MY rounds. I only spotted two of Murphy's guys, but you know how it goes with those guys. He kills them faster than we can identify them, so I'm sure some new guys were floating around there as well," I tell Cage.

"What was the purpose for staring at Serafina? To piss me off? Because it's working," Cage replies.

"I had a 'chat' with him. He may be big, but it's all show. He's not strong and he certainly isn't fast—physically or mentally."

"Big dumb oaf?" Sera asks.

I grin. "Yeah, exactly."

"So, he's pretty much 'eye candy' for Murphy like I pretend to be for Cage."

Cage's lips twitch. "That's one way of looking at it, but I certainly wouldn't call him candy."

"Well, no, not candy per se. He's more of a show piece, one made to intimidate," Sera elaborates.

"Yep. That's it. Nothing much up top," I reply.

"So, what's the game? With Murphy it's always a game," Cage states.

"Nicole."

"He came right out and told you that?" Sera asks.

"Yep. Sure did. He said they have nothing to hide."

"They were trying to intimidate us?" Sera laughs.

"Trying," I answer.

"They really don't know who they're messing with, do they?"

I give Sera a smirk. "No. They don't. They mustn't have done their homework since he called you Cage's 'side piece.'"

Sera laughs. "That's excellent. Let's keep everyone in the dark from the fact I'd shoot them between the eyes without blinking if they are a threat to any family of mine."

"And we've got a big family," I elaborate.

"We do," Cage agrees. "Tomorrow morning we'll work out a plan with Gio. See how we need to handle this."

I nod. "I'll leave you to it then."

"Thanks, Damian."

I nod again.

Sera gives me a hug and I pat her back lightly so as not to anger the lion that is her husband.

"See you in the morning," I tell them and walk out the door. I nod at the guards as I walk to my car.

I turn out of the drive and head for home. One day maybe I'll settle down. Maybe. If I do, it's going to be with a woman like Sera. I want someone I can share all aspects of my life with.

Maybe one day.

Chapter Seven

Lucy

I WAKE UP slowly, knowing there's no reason to rush. I remove my sleep mask and see it's dark outside. I'm not surprised, nor am I surprised that I'm still exhausted.

I look over at Jesse and he's out cold.

I slide out of bed and pad my way to the living area where my suitcase is. I unzip it and consider putting on a pretty bra and panties set, but should I? Will it be a waste?

No. Being sexy for my husband is never a waste. I grab the pink and black satin and lace set, the one Jesse loves so much, and make my way to the bathroom. The floor tile is cold and I need to pee. I do my business and decide to take a quick shower.

After whipping my hair up into a bun, I shower, enjoying the quiet, the solitude, the warm water washing over my skin. I relish this small reprieve from the world—even Jesse. I love him so much, but everyone needs time alone, and that's what I'm taking now. Time alone. Time for me.

If I'd thought to bring bath salts or oils, I'd have enjoyed the treat of a bath. I'll have to remember that for next time.

I'm still so tired. I've only slept about five hours. I need more.

So, after toweling myself dry, I slip on the pretty lingerie, let my hair fall down over my shoulders and back, then I carefully climb back into bed. I don't want to wake Jesse. Truthfully with the way he's snoring over there, I don't think I could.

I must have drifted off again because the next time I wake up, it's to Jesse coming out of the shower, drying his hair with a towel, wearing not a single stitch of clothes. Oh boy. Oh boy.

He sees me watching him and gives me a wink and a smile. Oh boy. Just that easily he turns me on. Just a look or a wink or the slightest touch. I know we're never going to lose that. Ever.

"Jesse," I rasp.

"Cupcake. Like what you see?" he teases.

"You know I do." I pull the sheet and blanket down to reveal myself to him and his smile immediately turns into a look of hunger. He licks his lips like he could eat me up. I certainly won't complain if he does. "You like?"

"Oh, I more than like." He stalks over, tossing the towel to the floor, just standing next to the bed staring at me. The only movement he makes is the clenching and unclenching of his fists. "You're like a present on Christmas morning. I don't know which part to unwrap first."

"Are you still tired?" I ask him.

"Yeah, but I really need to fuck my wife fast and hard, then we'll make slow lazy love. When we're done, we can nap again."

"Oh boy. That sounds perfect."

"I really like your lingerie, but I'm going to rip it off. I'll buy you some new stuff."

I'm already panting with want as he stands before me, his cock hard, droplets of water still sliding down his body. He's my walking wet dream. Literally.

True to his word, Jesse dives right in. He moves between my legs and sniffs my pussy through my panties.

"Christ, you smell good. I want to eat this pussy, but I'll wait until later. Right now I need to fuck you until you scream my name. There's no one to interrupt and no one to hear but me," he tells me with a glint in his eye. He grabs one side of my panties in both hands and pulls them apart with ease then repeats it on the same side.

"Oh boy." I can feel myself getting wetter, my heart racing, all at just the thought of my husband making good on his plans.

"You'll be more than 'oh boy-ing' in a few minutes. Cupcake, you're so beautiful I'm almost afraid to muss you—almost. I'm going to do all those things you like and then I'm going to do them again."

He unhooks my bra and I slip my arms out. Those deft fingers slip between my thighs to my pussy.

"You're so wet, baby. I fucking love it."

Then he stops touching and starts moving. First, he crawls up my body like a panther. Then he kisses my lips. Next, he grabs his cock and rubs it along my feminine folds, getting the head of his cock good and wet. I may have been with Jesse for more than three years, but it's still hard to take him inside me sometimes. The man is seriously well-endowed.

"Ready?" he asks.

"More than," I pant in reply.

Slowly he begins to fill me. Sliding in and out, feeding his cock into my pussy one inch at a time. Lord have mercy. Every time it feels like the first. It's so damn good.

"Fuck, you grip me so tight," Jesse groans when he's finally seated to the hilt. He pauses, letting me adjust.

"Jesse," I whisper, reaching up to cup his face in my hands.

"Fast and rough this time, Cupcake. Hold on," he warns.

Then he begins to move, and he wasn't kidding. He's fucking me hard and deep, getting a little faster with each thrust.

"Mmm," I moan.

Jesse reaches beneath me, holding my ass in his hands, then tilts my hips. Kablam! He hits the right spot and again and again and again. Over and over until I'm begging, pleading for him to give me what I need.

He's panting, sweat beading his forehead and upper lip, as he smirks down at me. "Already? So impatient."

"You said fast and har—omigod. Yes! There, right there!"

"I know where. Now give it to me. I want to feel your hot pussy tighten around my cock when you come all over it."

Oh, that dirty talking husband of mine.

He leans down and takes a nipple in his mouth, sucking hard, and thrusting just as hard and much faster now. I can feel his cock swelling even more and I know he's close. I lift and lower my hips to meet him and within three seconds I'm coming. I scream out his name, my body shaking and shuddering.

"Fuuuuuck," Jesse moans as he comes. His orgasm prolongs mine and I'm finding it hard to breathe.

"Jesse!"

"That's right. No one fucks you like I do. No one ever will," he mutters.

"Omigod, Jesse," I moan when he slows his movements.

"Damn straight. We needed that," Jesse tells me, looking down into my face with such love in his eyes, I feel it in my soul.

I nod. "We did. I really hate screaming into the pillow."

Jesse chuckles. "You can be as loud as you want here, Cupcake. I love hearing you. The noises you make, and that hip swivel thing you did. I nearly shot my load."

"Like that, did ya? I was trying something new."

"It was fucking amazing."

"Let's do it again," I tell him.

"Slow this time. I want to savor you, make you come three or four times. Then we can take a nap."

He leans in and kisses me so softly, like a butterfly wings touching my lips at first. It's not long before his hips start moving again, his kiss more passionate, and I thank God for this man who not only tells me he loves me but also shows me by all-but worshiping my body as he makes love to me.

"I love you so much, Jesse."

"There aren't words to describe it for me, Lucy."

I still thank my lucky stars and wonder how it came to be that my childhood crush became my happily-ever-after. I hold him tight and love him right back.

Chapter Eight

Sera

WHEN DAMIAN LEAVES, I give Cage some space to work things out in his head. I can see the tension and the worry he has about this Murphy asshat. I vow that no one will hurt our Coley. No one. I'll kill them before they even get close. She's fought too hard to beat the C word and now she's got such an amazing family. Why can't life stop messing with her?

I sigh as I remove my clothes and put on my silk robe that hits me mid-thigh. In the bathroom, I remove my makeup and wash my face, still thinking of that hulk of a man. His stares would have had most women afraid. Me? I just wanted to kick his ass. How dare he try to intimidate me? I'm positive it was because I was a woman. He didn't stare at Cage like that. Sexist bastard. He'll find out. When the time comes, he'll be the one who's intimidated.

I sigh again. The amount of bullshit we've had to put up with hasn't been too much, considering we're the mafia or the mob or whatever you want to call it. I account that to us being solid. Strong. People don't want to mess with the Russos—and they shouldn't. We are a force to be reckoned with.

I slide into bed in my lavender silk nightie. I don't really consider it a negligee. I just love the silky feel against my skin when I'm sleeping, though most of the time I wake up in just my panties. I sleep on top of Cage, literally on top of him, and somehow he gets me topless every night. Some nights he manages to get the panties off too. The devil.

I start reading the latest indie novel from Harper Bentley. Those Powers Boys. Yum!

I'm engrossed in the book when Cage comes in—with his glasses on. Holy smokes. Sometimes I can't believe he's my husband. He's so good looking it should be illegal. I'm not even kidding. I think part of the appeal is his quiet, cool confidence.

He catches me staring. I don't even care. This is the kind of stare that's legit. I'm leering at my man. Now, he lifts his brows and his lips twitch.

I push the blankets down and half crawl-half lay across the bed, then turn onto my back, my arms raised above my head.

"I've been waiting for you."

"Really. I thought the Powers boys would entertain you enough."

"Baby, you're not really jealous of fictional college boys, are you?" I tease.

This time only one brow lifts as if to ask, "Are you serious?" As if this man would be jealous. He's possessive, yes; but he knows I'm his one hundred and fifty percent. He's secure in our love as am I.

"Everything okay?" I ask as he unbuttons his dress shirt.

He nods. "I just don't like this new development. This needs to be handled swiftly or there'll be consequences."

I sit up on my knees, my legs folded beneath me. "We've got the best of the best which means we'll do our best. That's all we can do, love."

"I know, Fee," he replies as he takes off his socks. "I'm just edgy."

I've never known Cage to be edgy. Not even when the Manzini's threatened their worst. I don't know how to help him with this.

Well, maybe I do.

"Come here, my love," I beckon, rubbing the spot on the bed where he sleeps.

He smirks and his eyes darken.

"On your front. Let me give you a massage."

He lets out what can only be described as a grunt, then lays flat as instructed.

I reach over to my bedside table and pick up my lotion.

"You're going to smell like honeysuckle," I tease.

"I'll smell like you. I'll smell even more like you before the night's through," Cage replies.

I rub my thighs together in anticipation. Just a few words—promises to be sure—from my husband has me aroused.

I straddle his buttocks and sit.

"I prefer to be the one on top in this position," he teases.

"Later."

"Count on it."

I warm the lotion in my hands before applying it to his back, spreading it outward, digging my thumbs deep into the muscles, eliciting a groan from between Cage's weary lips.

I work his shoulders, and downward to his lower back, working out the knots along the way.

"Fee," he murmurs.

"Cage?"

"That was perfect, but I've got other aches now."

I smirk. "Is that so?"

"Don't you ache?" he asks. "For me? Having had your hands all over my body for the last thirty minutes?"

"I ache for you when you walk into a room."

"Your turn. As much as I love your silk, you need to remove it, then lay on your front," he commands. His tone—it's that tone. The dominant one. The one he saves for me in the bedroom. The one he knows I crave.

I obey—naturally. When he commands me, it's instinctual for me to immediately do as he says. We are a fluid pair.

He rubs the lotion between his hands as he straddles my ass, holding his weight on his knees, before lowering those large masculine hands to my back and gently kneading my tired muscles.

I moan. "That feels incredible."

"Mmm, yes you do."

His hands glide over my skin like the silk I just removed. Never too hard, even when he finds tension.

"Let's remove these, shall we," Cage murmurs when those talented fingers reach my panties.

"Yes, I do think we shall," I agree, lifting my hips in hopes he won't rip them. I really like this pair. He rips them anyway, a rare display of impatience from my calm, cool, and controlled man I love.

He touches between my legs, his fingers running through my wet feminine folds, rubbing lightly on my clit, sensitive and ready for more.

"I love how wet you are."

"Only for you."

He lowers himself over me, his arms on either side of my shoulders, his mouth at my ear when he whispers, "Are you ready for me, wife?"

"Always. I'm always ready for you." And I am. Anytime, anywhere. It only takes his presence, a word, a look, and I'm drenched and longing for him.

He moves down then spreads my legs. When I move to go up on my knees, he merely holds his hand on my lower back to stay the motion.

"No. Like this."

His large frame covers mine, his elbows and knees taking most of his weight. Within seconds he's pushing his hard cock inside me, slowly, steadily, and I can't hold back the moan. It feels too good. Every single time he's inside me, I unravel.

He threads his fingers through mine, raising them above my head, his breath wafting over a sensitive spot on my neck—not by chance either. No. My husband knows everything about my body and he uses it to his advantage. I appreciate it. I admire it. I love it.

He begins to move at a quicker pace, just as I knew he would. He needs this. He needs me. He needs us to help clear out the weight of the world and find some peace.

"Tell me how it feels," he demands.

"Fabulous. Decadent. So damn good."

"All of the above," he agrees, quickening his thrusts just a bit more, giving me just enough room to lift and lower against him.

"Fee," he breathes into my ear.

I tighten my hold on his fingers.

"Knees," he commands just before taking our linked hands, putting them beneath my abdomen to help sit me up. I expected just knees, but he aligns our bodies, both of us on our knees, sitting on our feet as we lift and lower together.

"You're so deep," I cry out.

"Too much?"

"No, no. Just right."

The pleasure has spread. He takes our hands and places them over my breasts, tweaking my nipples, as we move even faster.

"Faster," I murmur. I want more. I need everything.

"Yes. Faster."

His right hand continues to fondle my breast, while the left reaches down between my legs to rub his index finger over my clit.

"No, please," I beg. "It's too much."

His balls slapping against my clit feel better than his fingers, so he repositions them over my hip, guiding my movements as he thrusts harder and harder.

I lift my arms above my head to wrap them around him behind me.

"I feel you. So hot and wet. You're so close."

"Almost…" I mutter as the flutters begin.

The pleasure is right there, within my grasp. I reach for it and he meets me half way, giving me just what I need. With one more hard thrust, the pleasure multiples, stealing my breath. My pussy clenching around him as he slows his thrusts, groaning with each pulse of his orgasm, his cum splashing inside me.

He turns us to our sides, still inside me. I don't want him to slip free just yet. Afraid he might, I control my breathing as best as I can.

"I'm ovulating," I blurt out.

He continues with the motion of pushing the hair out of my face. "Are you sure you're ready? I know you said you were on New Year's, but we haven't discussed it."

"I haven't been on birth control for two months. I want us to have a baby. I want to have our child growing inside me—a part of you," I confess softly.

"The best parts of us," he adds.

I nod, letting a tear fall.

"Are you sure?" I ask.

"Yes. And before you ask, it's not because you want it. I want it too. With you. I want everything with you, Fee," he professes, tightening his hold on me.

"I love you so much, Cage. With everything in me."

"I love you, Fee. With all that I am. Always and forever."

I smile. "Only ever you."

Chapter Nine

Jesse

"THAT WAS ONE of the best times of my life," I tell Lucy. She looks at me confused. "Just you and me. No rush. No hurry. No being quiet. Just you and me, fucking, loving, sleeping, holding one another, not needing to say a word because we both just know."

"Oh, Jesse. I loved this. We need to do this more. We don't need to reconnect, because we're always connected. That's not what this was about for me. I just needed to recharge my batteries. I just needed some you-and-me time. Just us."

He nods. "Me too."

We're both silent as we're driven to CFD.

Jesse chuckles. "I bet those four gave them a run for their money."

I laugh. "God, I hope so. Let them see what nearly twenty-four hours of four toddlers is like."

"We should stop for lunch before we head home." I just want some more time alone with my wife. She's beautiful. So beautiful.

"We should," she agrees with a pleased smile.

You did good there, Kingston. I love my wife happy.

I tell the driver to take us to a quiet restaurant we enjoy.

Lucy leans into my side, taking my hand in her small ones.

"Let's enjoy these last couple hours together."

"Nothing would make me happier," she replies with a gleam in her eye. "Because my husband is handsome and sexy and delicious in bed. He's my rock, my partner in all things, and I love him more than life itself."

"Cupcake," I murmur, leaning in to kiss her softly, lingeringly. "Everything you just said?"

She nods.

"All of that and I look forward to spending the next fifty, maybe sixty years with you," I tell her.

"Oh, Jesse."

I kiss her all the way to the restaurant, and when we step out, my heart skips a beat when she looks at me with so much love in her eyes. And it's all for me.

I'm one lucky bastard.

Chapter Ten

Cage

"WHAT DO YOU think's going to happen?" Sera asks as she buttons her jeans.

"I know what I'd like to happen, but it'd be impulsive. That's not good business," I answer honestly.

"I want him dead too."

She knows. She always knows.

"He'll get there, and we'll be the ones to put him there. Until then we keep our family safe."

"And trust no one," Sera replies.

I nod. "Only Famiglia."

She hugs me tight. "He won't get to them. We won't let them."

"No, we won't. But, Fee, when you're pregnant, you can not be in the line of fire." Her temper flares in her eyes. "I won't apologize to you for making this rule as second. Gio will make it if I don't."

"I'm aware," she bites out, turning away. "I wouldn't ever put our child in harm's way. You should know me better than that. You should also know how much I hate being told what I can or can not do."

This woman. So incredible. So invigorating. So frustrating.

"I'm aware," I bite back, using her tone. "I don't like having to make rules, but it's my duty."

She snorts.

"Putting duty aside, you're my wife. That would be my child. I trust you. I know you'd never put him or her in the line of danger. I just have to follow the rules, Fee. I'd rather do that in private than when we arrive at the meeting with everyone around us," I disclose.

She turns and looks at me now. Such a gorgeous face. Such a beautiful soul.

"How long did you stay up worrying about this?" she questions.

"I didn't. I worked it out before I came to bed."

She nods then walks to me and wraps her arms around me, resting her head on my chest.

"We're okay?" I question.

"We're always okay, Cage."

I hold her close. "Good. Now we make sure everyone else stays that way too."

THE END.

Did you enjoy PULSE? Please consider leaving a review.

Acknowledgments

Wow, I have so many people to thank.

Tons of thanks to all of you, the readers, for sticking with me through the rough times.

To the members of the Facebook La Famiglia group—I adore you. Every day you make me smile. I feel like the luckiest person/author ever. I have the best readers and friends EVER!

Super thanks to the bloggers. You are marvelous! You are invaluable. You promote me and my books so selflessly—words will never be enough to thank you.

To the Sparkly Ladies, my beta group: Anita, Jennifer, Joanne, Keisha, Lisa, Loretta, Mandi, Melissa, Nina, Penny, Sophie, and Tianna! –Your feedback and help are priceless. Thank you for being available at odd hours to give me your thoughts and opinions talking me down from the ledge.

Thank you, Mom, for always reminding me why I do what I do.

To Mandi Wathey—My sister from another mister: I adore you. Thank you so much for unwavering support and love.

To Nicole Bailey—You're more than my editor. You're my friend. My title brainstormer. My go-to person when I'm feeling unsure. You're honest and forthright and I couldn't appreciate that more! I can't imagine my life without you! I can't imagine writing a book without you!

To Melissa Mendoza—my amazing personal assistant and friend. For all you do, words will never be enough. I value you and everything you do for me and with me. I value our working relationship and our friendship. I love that we can have both.

I'm positive I'm forgetting people and for that I'm sorry.

Playlist

PULSE—a #JUCY and #SAGE short story

Safe and Sound—Julia Sheer
Undone—Hailey Reinhart
You—The Pretty Reckless
I Can't Not Love You—Every Avenue
Anywhere But Here—SafetySuit
Bring On The Rain—Jo Dee Messina
She Is Love—Parachute
Unlike Any Other—Delta Rae
Edge of Desire—John Mayer
Bad Intentions—Niykee Heaton
Sugar—Maroon 5
Never Stop—SafetySuit
Next To Me—Emeli Sandé
Make You Miss Me—Sam Hunt
Loveliest Thing—Jaymes Reunion
I Won't Let You Go—James Morrison
I Found In You—Sarah Darling
All of Me—Jason Chen, Madilyn Bailey
Kiss Me Slowly—Parachute
Meant To Be—Parachute
Not A Bad Thing—Justin Timberlake
Best I Can—Art of Dying
Easy To Love You—Theory of a Deadman
Brown Eyed Girl—Van Morrison
Never Be The Same—Red
Your Song—Elton John
Shock The Monkey—Coal Chamber

Other Available Titles

About the Author

Anne Mercier is the author of the bestselling Rockstar series, The Way series, Truths series, and Forbidden Fantasies series. She writes multiple genres to include contemporary adult erotic romance, contemporary adult romance, new adult romance, and mature young adult romance.

She grew up in Wisconsin and still lives there today. She's an avid reader who gets inspired by reading stories from her favorite authors as well as listening to various types of music. Anne is a huge fan of music, chocolate, fruit, desserts, autumn, M. Shadows, Avenged Sevenfold, and Milo Ventimiglia.

Through her books, she is proudly creating new Avenged Sevenfold and Milo Ventimiglia fans one reader at a time.

Made in the USA
Lexington, KY
23 January 2019